Amish Winter of Hope

The Amish Bonnet Sisters Book #14

Samantha Price

Chapter 1

Hope sat alone at the kitchen table, slowly buttering her toast so she didn't miss any spots. She didn't like biting into dry toast at all. Once the butter had melted nicely, she dolloped on a big spoonful of honey. Then she took her knife and spread the honey into a thick layer that completely covered the toast. All the while, she was deep in thought about the first time she ever saw Fairfax. He had literally knocked on the door of her family's home. He'd been looking for Florence for some reason or other. It had been love at first sight for her, and he'd said later it had been the same for him.

Hope had been the last into the kitchen this morning. Everyone had finished breakfast and now they were huddled around the fireplace in the living room keeping warm. All of them, that was, except for Bliss, who was making clattering sounds while she washed up.

The noises didn't bother Hope; she barely noticed them. What she did notice was the smell of baking bread, and that was odd for a Sunday when cooking was to be kept to a minimum. That meant Hope was now eating the last of the bread, and her mother, whose job was the bread-making, had been unorganized in the last couple of days.

Perhaps it wasn't *Mamm's* fault. Maybe someone had suddenly eaten a lot more bread than normal.

For Hope, Sunday was the day of the week she looked forward to. Not only was it their day of rest, it was when she got to spend the most time with Fairfax.

Today there was no meeting, so she could spend the whole afternoon with him and she hoped he'd talk more about their future. There were so many things to decide upon. When they would marry, where they would live, and where he would work.

Lately, he hadn't talked about such things and Hope feared there was a reason for that.

Was it possible he was having second thoughts? She hadn't wanted to let that fearful thought take hold of her, but it had increased with every passing day.

He'd finished the instructions, and been baptized, so why was he still living and working with the Millers?

If only the bishop hadn't placed him with a family that owned a dairy farm. It hadn't been easy for him. Working the dairy was not an easy task and everyone knew it. She could tell when she looked at Fairfax that he was sleep-deprived and exhausted most of the time. No one made good choices or thought properly when they lacked sleep.

Although the Millers had told Fairfax they'd like him to stay on permanently, he'd politely declined and informed them he would prefer to return to orchard work. Yet, after he'd said that he was still with the Millers—living and working with them.

Hope hadn't asked Florence and Carter yet, but she was certain they'd have work for him. They'd purchased Fairfax's parents' orchard that was on one side of the Baker

Apple Orchard, and they were creating a new orchard on their land on the other side of the Baker Orchard. They were always employing people to do things around the place, so why not employ Fairfax instead? He already knew what was necessary and how to do what needed doing to run the place.

It made sense to Hope and she knew it would make sense to her half-sister, Florence, too.

The only thing was, she didn't want to be the one to ask them and it disappointed her that Fairfax hadn't made any inquiries.

Hope continued to eat her toast and thought some more.

She'd often wondered if she should whisper a hint to Florence, but each time she'd decided against it. Fairfax should be bold enough to do that himself. How could he support himself and her after they married if he had no job and nowhere to live?

It had become an ongoing worry for her. Fairfax wasn't a planner like she was, and she found that frustrating.

Life had to be planned.

Weddings had to be organized, and their life together had to be thought out.

It wasn't just going to tumble together with no thought and no effort.

No one was going to knock on Fairfax's door and give him a job and a place to live. If he stayed with the Millers, she'd never see him, and their lives would never go ahead. It would make no sense to marry if he was still working with the Millers. There was no room for her in the quarters he shared with another of the dairy's workers. It would be an awful way to begin their married life.

"Hope."

Hope looked up to see Bliss leaning over her. "What is it?" Hope asked.

"What are you thinking about?"

"Fairfax."

"Oh, it's so good to be in love, isn't it?"

She looked up at Bliss, envying her for the very first time. Adam Wengerd was the man Bliss loved. He was someone to admire, and he was a planner. He'd started his own business when he couldn't find permanent work, and had moved communities to be close to Bliss. By the time Bliss and Adam married, they'd have a house and a plan for their lives. Hope was certain of that because Adam was someone who followed through with the decisions he made.

All Hope wanted was some idea of the path she and Fairfax were taking.

Bliss had none of the worries that she was having right now. Maybe Fairfax was like this because he was concentrating on doing the right thing in the right way, community-wise. Or it might have been because that was just the way he was.

"*Jah,* Bliss. Love is good," Hope finally said.

"Do you want another cup of coffee? I'm having one."

"Okay, *denke.*"

Minutes later, Bliss passed her a cup and sat down opposite her. "What's the matter?"

"Nothing." Hope traced her fingertip along the wood grain in the table. "Why do you think something's the matter?"

"You look sad and gloomy."

"I'm not. I've just got a lot on my mind."
She wouldn't share her fears with Bliss. Not
when Bliss looked up to her as the older
sister. They'd all had too much uncertainty
in their lives of late, with Levi's illness and
the ongoing uncertainty that surrounded
the orchard. Hope didn't want to add
another layer of worry, no matter how small.

"Are you seeing Fairfax today?" Bliss
asked.

"*Jah*. He said he'd be here about lunchtime
and then we'd do something together. I'm
not sure what."

"I'm not seeing Adam until he comes for
dinner tonight."

"I'll invite Fairfax for dinner too. Oh, sorry
about you not seeing him this morning or
this afternoon. I know you haven't seen
him much lately."

"*Jah,* he's been working long hours." Bliss sighed, just as Cherish walked into the kitchen and sat down heavily next to Bliss.

Then Cherish got back to her feet and headed to Timmy in his cage. "Who's a pretty boy? Who's a pretty boy?"

It was impossible to talk while Cherish was around.

"Oh, he's not talking now." Cherish swung around. "It's because you two are here."

Bliss asked, "Does he talk when no one's around?"

"A little. He makes noises like he's trying to say the words, but it's not very clear. I was sure he'd be able to talk by now." She turned around to face Timmy. "Pretty boy, pretty boy." She gave up and sat down next to Bliss. Then she put her elbows on the table and rested her head in her hands. "I'm so bored. There's nothing to do." Her head lowered to the table. "Why is life so boring? Sundays are always like this."

Today, Hope was in no mood to put up with Cherish and her dramatics.

Once Hope had finished her toast and coffee, she headed up to her room, and there she'd stay until Fairfax arrived.

Cherish asked Bliss, "What's wrong with her? She didn't even look at me."

"I don't know. She seems a little odd today."

"Did I do something to upset her?"

Bliss leaned back in the chair. "I don't think you did anything, but you were a bit noisy when we were having a conversation. What are you doing today?"

Cherish ignored her and stared at Bliss's coffee cup. "Oh, you've got coffee."

Bliss jumped to her feet. "Want me to make you one?"

"*Jah.* That would be good."

As Bliss poured the coffee out of the carafe, she said, "Why didn't you get one at breakfast?"

"I don't know. I don't normally have much, but it feels like a coffee-drinking day today. I have nothing planned. I have no one to visit and no one to visit me. All my friends told me they're busy today and all of my sisters have boyfriends except for Favor." Cherish heaved another sigh. "But Favor has her time all taken up by Caroline. I mean, why is *she* still even here? No one can give me an answer." Cherish pouted. "I should tell Levi the truth about her house. Tell him it didn't burn down at all and that she's a liar. Everyone knows it. Except for Levi and of course *Mamm.*"

"Wunderbaar."

Cherish looked at Bliss in surprise. "It's *wunderbaar* that we have a liar as a guest?"

"Nee, it's *wunderbaar* that we can do something together today. Just the two of us."

Cherish thought about that. She'd rather do something with Favor than with Bliss, but Favor and Caroline had disappeared after breakfast and she wasn't even sure where they were. *"Jah,* okay. What did you have in mind?" At this stage, doing something was better than doing nothing.

"I don't know. I want to put Cottonball in her enclosure for a while. She loves to chew on the grass and nuzzle around in the dirt. It's too cold this morning. I'll wait until this afternoon. She doesn't even notice the cold with all that fur. I like to watch her while she's in there to make sure she's okay."

"If you want to do something this morning, I'll watch Cottonball with you this afternoon."

"Okay. What do you want to do?" Bliss brought the cup of coffee back to the table and placed it in front of Cherish.

Cherish opened her mouth to answer but was distracted by loud voices coming from the living room. It was *Mamm* and Levi. "What are they talking about?"

Bliss shrugged her shoulders. "I don't like the sound of it. *Dat* seems upset and when he was at the hospital, they said he wasn't to get stressed."

"I know—he has to remain calm."

Mamm was the culprit. It sounded like she was arguing with him.

Chapter 2

Levi's voice was louder than normal and hinted of irritation. *"Nee.* Why would you invite Ada and Samuel for our meeting with Florence and Carter? It's got nothing to do with them."

"It's done and it's too late. I've already asked them. I thought I mentioned it before. I'm sure I did."

"Nee. I would've remembered. Why would you do this, Wilma?"

"So they can listen too, and tell us what they think."

"You can uninvite them, Wilma. This has nothing to do with them. It's between us and Carter and Florence."

"I can't uninvite them. They're our friends. They might have some good suggestions that we haven't thought about. Don't you want to hear what they think?"

Levi's voice got slower and more controlled. "This is nothing about them. They can come for dinner and come to our *haus* as much as you want, but not tomorrow. I'll hitch the buggy and you can go over now and tell them that yourself."

Bliss, listening from the kitchen was worried. *"Dat* shouldn't upset himself after his heart attack."

"I know. You said that."

"What should I do? Should I go out there?" Bliss whispered to Cherish.

Cherish was concerned, too. "You can't do anything. He has to sort things out with *Mamm*."

They both got up from the table, and stood by the door to listen.

They heard Wilma say, *"Ach,* I can't uninvite them. You do it. You're the one that doesn't want them here."

"Nee, Wilma. I can, but I won't. You didn't even ask me if they could come."

"I never usually ask," Wilma whined.

"This is different. We're talking about the ownership of the orchard. I'm doing my best to fix another of your mistakes."

Cherish and Bliss looked at one another. *Mamm* and Levi were having a full-blown argument.

Although Cherish didn't say it, she knew her mother wanted someone else at that meeting, maybe someone who would be on her side? She didn't think she'd be supported by her husband and she was probably right, going by how he was reacting.

Wilma said, "I'll do it, but I'll get one of the girls to hitch the buggy. You should still be resting."

"I've had enough rest. I'm not dead yet. I feel fine. I can do simple things like hitch a buggy."

"Okay. Suit yourself. You normally do anyway. No consideration for my feelings or the feelings of my dear friend."

Bliss couldn't stand there and listen any longer. She hurried into the living room. *"Dat,* I'll hitch the buggy for *Mamm."*

Cherish walked out behind her. "I'll help too."

Wilma and Levi looked up at the two girls, seeming surprised.

Bliss frowned at her father. "Just please don't say more about being dead. It's too upsetting."

"I won't. I didn't know you were listening. It seems you both were." Levi looked from one to the other, but he didn't seem upset by their sudden appearance.

Wilma stood up and fixed her fists on her hips. "Were you two eavesdropping just now? It's not good if you were. You're both old enough to know better."

"You're right, *Mamm,*" Cherish said. "We were listening, but we weren't doing it deliberately ... it wasn't on purpose."

"I don't believe you. Just for that, you can both go to her house and tell her not to come tomorrow afternoon."

Cherish gulped. The last thing she wanted was to face Ada, particularly when she was delivering unwelcome news. "And by 'her,' you mean Ada?"

"*Jah*. That's right. Tell her there was a misunderstanding about our meeting tomorrow, not to come visit us tomorrow at all, and I'll talk with her Tuesday."

"Okay."

"Unless I see her before that," *Mamm* added.

Cherish inhaled deeply and then looked over at Bliss. "Come on, Bliss."

"I'd go myself," Wilma said, "but I'm waiting for the bread to bake. Wait. It's not necessary for both of you to go."

"Wilma, just let the girls go together. I don't like just one of them traveling too far. The world's not safe in these times. I'd rather they go in pairs."

Wilma stuck her nose in the air. "It's not far." When Levi gave her 'the look' she turned to the girls and snapped, "Just hurry, then."

Cherish grabbed Bliss's arm and took their coats from the peg by the front door, then they both walked as fast as they could out of the house.

Bliss pulled on her coat as they headed to the paddock to get one of the buggy horses. "I'm worried that *Mamm* and *Dat* aren't getting along."

"Don't worry about it. They'll be fine. They'll be all better when this thing with the orchard is sorted."

Bliss swung around. "Will it ever be? It's been going on for so long now."

"*Jah.* That's what they're doing tomorrow. Sorting it all out for good. I heard Levi tell *Mamm* he's got some ideas to put to Florence and Carter."

"Okay. I hope you're right."

"I mostly am."

"Except when you're wrong."

"You're funny today, Bliss." Cherish laughed and then Bliss put up her hand.

"Stay there. I'll get him." Bliss walked slowly to the horse and slipped a rope around his neck. Then she patted his shoulder. "Good boy, Charlie."

Cherish walked over and patted Charlie's neck. "Yeah, good boy, Charlie. You're *wunderbaar* with horses, Bliss. You're just like your *vadder.*"

"They can sense I like them. They pick up on feelings. When someone's afraid of them, they get afraid too. That's when they can act out, but if you're calm and confident around them, it makes them feel good and safe. In the wild, if they're afraid they can gallop away, but they can't do that in captivity. They do other things and then they're labeled as too wild, but they're not really. They just haven't been treated with respect."

"If you say so."

"I do. I mean, they can't gallop away, so they might strike out at someone or rear up."

"I get it. I never really thought about it."

Cherish hurried to open the gate and Bliss led Charlie out of the paddock. They were both silent while they strapped the harness bits and bobs to the horse and then fitted the buggy to it.

When they climbed into the buggy, Bliss grabbed the reins. Whomever was the oldest normally drove the horse and buggy. That way there was no arguing about whose turn it was.

They headed down the driveway, past the shop where they spotted Caroline and Favor, and turned onto the road.

"Caroline and Favor are using the shop as their personal living room," Bliss said, with a laugh.

"Suits me. With them out of the way I get to sit closer to the fire. It's better when there are less people to huddle around it." Cherish grabbed two blankets from the back seat. She spread one over herself and spread the other over Bliss.

"Denke. This will be a bit awkward, to uninvite Ada. I hope she doesn't ask too many probing questions. I think *Dat* would prefer keeping things to himself."

"About the orchard, you mean?"

"Jah," Bliss said.

"No chance of that. *Mamm* tells Ada everything. Wait, she didn't tell her about hiding *Dat's* will, and that really surprised me. So, *Mamm* can keep some things quiet when it suits her to do it."

Half an hour later, they pulled the horse and buggy up in front of Samuel and Ada's large house.

Cherish had jumped out before Bliss had fully stopped. "Hello Ada and Samuel," she said when she saw them relaxing on chairs on their porch. "Isn't it too cold to be out here?"

"We're enjoying the morning sun while it lasts. The weather can be so unpredictable lately. What brings both of you out to visit us? Don't you have some folks your own ages you can visit?"

"*Nee*, well, we do but—"

Ada stood up and folded her arms across her chest while Samuel stayed seated. "I know what this is about."

"Do you?" Cherish asked.

Bliss had secured the horse and now she was standing beside Cherish while they both looked up at Ada.

"*Jah*. You're after an answer about whether we'll go with you to the farm."

A smile lit Cherish's face. "That's not why we're here, but have you talked about it?"

Ada turned around and exchanged a grin with her husband. "We will, in the warmer weather. In the springtime."

Cherish did her best to hide her disappointment. They were talking about a good six months' wait. She had hoped to go soon, before Christmas or just after at the very latest. "Thank you, both. I appreciate that."

"That's not why we're here," Bliss told them.

Samuel moved to stand beside his wife. "Is it your *vadder*, Bliss?"

"*Nee. Dat's* fine, by the grace of *Gott*, but I'm here about tomorrow afternoon and the meeting *Mamm* and *Dat* are having with Carter and Florence."

"*Jah*, the one about the orchard. I already told Wilma we'll be there."

Cherish was glad it was Bliss doing the talking.

"You see ..." Bliss looked at Cherish, searching for words, hoping for some help. But she was met with a blank stare. "*Mamm* and *Dat* will be talking to Florence and Carter about the arrangements for the orchard tomorrow afternoon, and they've decided it should be just between the four of them."

Samuel slowly nodded.

"Who decided this?" Ada snapped. "Wilma said I could come only yesterday. It was she who wanted me to come. Now, she doesn't want me to come? Or, is it Levi who doesn't want me there?"

Cherish froze, and now Bliss was staring at her and waiting for her to speak.

Chapter 3

"They both agreed about it," Cherish finally blurted out.

"Who, Florence and Carter?" asked Ada.

Cherish shook her head. She couldn't let Ada know that it was Levi who thought they shouldn't be there. *"Nee, not them."*

"I see. The truth is plain to see. As plain as the nose on your face, Cherish."

Cherish's fingertips touched her nose. Was there something wrong with it? Here she was worried about her sallow skin and the dark circles under her eyes when all the time she should've been concerned about her ugly nose. Why hadn't someone else said something?

"It's only reasonable for us not to be there, Ada," Samuel said. "It really has nothing to do with us. I'd rather not be there when people are discussing their personal and financial matters."

"Still, I'm sure Wilma needs me there. She always asks my advice about things. This doesn't sound like the Wilma I know."

Cherish held up her hands. "I'm sorry." She didn't know what else to say.

"No need for you or anyone to be sorry. It's just not a good idea to do things like that."

Ada looked at Samuel. "What's that? Do things like what?"

"A group discussion. Someone's always got a different opinion. Someone needs to take charge and say what's happening. That's the best idea."

"Maybe so," Bliss said. Then she looked at Cherish. "Should we go now?"

"Yes. That's all we came to say."

"Short and sweet," Ada said through gritted teeth. "Won't you at least come in and have some tea with us? Hot tea to warm you on a cool day."

"It has been quite cold in the buggy. I'd love a cup, *denke,*" said Bliss.

What? Cherish couldn't believe Bliss. She was sure Bliss would want to get out of there too. Ada would pump them for more information and get more upset that she was being left out. Now, a good part of the day would be wasted. A day, the only day of the week when she didn't have to suffer over chores, and here they were, stuck with Ada and Samuel. They weren't even driving her to the farm for another half year, six whole months. "We can't stay long, though," Cherish announced when Samuel pulled forward two chairs for them to sit in.

"Can we go inside?" Bliss asked, rubbing her shoulders. "Not much point drinking hot tea to warm us when we're sitting on the cold front porch."

Bliss was right. Didn't they know it was winter?

Samuel laughed. "You're coming out of your shell, Bliss."

Ada turned around at the doorway. "You never normally would speak out like that."

"I've been teaching her to speak her mind," Cherish said.

"Well, it's good to see that you're doing some good."

Cherish ignored Ada's sarcastic comment. There was no point replying.

Bliss continued to rub her arms. "It's cold out here and it would be so much warmer inside in front of the fire."

"We will appreciate the warmth when we go inside later." Ada pressed her lips together. "Come inside with me, Bliss. You can help me bring out the tea items. You can stay here with Samuel, Cherish. You can both talk about ... whatever you want to talk about."

"Very well." Cherish sat on one of the chairs Samuel had got from the side of the porch. It seemed they were staying right there in the cold. Yes the sun was out, but it was doing nothing to warm them. "How are things, Samuel?"

Samuel chuckled. "I still can't get used to you girls calling me Samuel. It wasn't so long ago it was *Onkel* Samuel."

"*Jah*, well, you're not my *onkel*."

"I know, but it reminds me how much you girls are growing up. It's sad really."

"Sad? What would be sad is if we stayed young and never grew up. It would be like an illness."

"*Jah*, not for parents. Ada and I have had an empty home for some time now. Our *kinner* have all moved away as you know. It's lonely for us and soon it'll be the same for Levi and your *mudder*."

"I guess so, but I'm sure *Mamm* will love the quiet and there'd be less work too. She's always complaining about having to clean up after us."

"You'll be going to the farm to live when you're older. Your *mudder* has told us how you've hurt her feelings by reminding her of that at every chance you can get."

"She's told you that?"

"Jah."

"I don't mean to hurt her feelings. It's just a fact."

"I know that. But it can still hurt someone. Maybe she thinks you're using that to get at her."

"Maybe." Cherish wanted to say that her mother should've thought of that before she sent her away to stay with Aunt Dagmar, but she thought that sounded rude. Anyway, she hadn't come here to be corrected by Samuel or told how to behave. At that moment, Ada came out with a tray of tea with Bliss following her holding a big plate of cookies.

"Ada, are they your chocolate chip cookies?" Cherish asked.

"*Jah,* baked fresh yesterday."

"Although, they do taste better when they're a few weeks old," Samuel said.

Cherish made a face. She didn't know about that. Old cookies were stale cookies. Perhaps he had false teeth or something and couldn't bite into fresh ones.

Once they were all seated with a cup of tea each, Ada asked, "What else is happening at your *haus?*" She looked at Cherish and then looked at Bliss.

"Nothing really," Cherish said. "It's just a normal day."

"Now that Fairfax is baptized he'll be marrying Hope, won't he?" Ada asked. "Wasn't that the plan? Wilma hasn't said anything, but she's been wondering some things."

Cherish knew she meant that Wilma had indeed said something.

"*Jah,* but Hope's too young, isn't she, surely?" Samuel asked. "She's not even twenty yet."

Cherish scratched her chin and looked down. "No one tells me their plans."

"*Jah,* but that's why he's joined us. So, it won't be long. I think we'll have a winter wedding." Ada looked upward blinking. "They're leaving things very late. When I was young, most of the weddings were in the wintertime after the harvest. Now, they're year-round, it seems."

Cherish glanced at Bliss and knew she was about to giggle. Once Bliss started it was hard for her to stop. Cherish picked up the plate of cookies and offered one to Bliss. "Have one."

Bliss was careful not to make eye-contact with anyone as she grabbed a cookie, and mumbled, *"Denke."*

"Oh, I do wish I could be with Wilma while decisions are being made about the orchard. She looks to me for advice."

"We'll find out soon enough what they decide," said Samuel.

"I know. I'll visit Wilma later today, that is, if I'm allowed."

Bliss started shaking, and Cherish had to talk. "Of course. *Mamm* will love to see you. Will you be coming too, Samuel?"

"Jah. I'll visit. I'll be the one doing the driving."

"Good."

Ada narrowed her eyes at Bliss. "Have I said something funny?"

That made Bliss worse. "I'm sorry." Bliss set her tea cup down along with the cookie and ran to the buggy.

Ada and Samuel stared after her, craning their necks as she ran to where they'd left the buggy. Cherish was looking too, but once Bliss was safely in the buggy, Cherish turned to face them.

"I'm sorry about her," Cherish said. "She's not been herself since Levi had his heart attack. Don't be upset with her. She means nothing by it."

"Has she gone mad?" Ada asked.

"It's quite possible, I suppose. Once she laughs like that, it's best not to say anything because it makes her shake and she can't talk."

"It's very odd. Should she go to a doctor?"

"No. Not at all. It's just nerves."

"Nerves can be a problem." Samuel looked at Ada. "What do you think?"

"I think the girl needs to be watched closely. There could be something wrong with her. She could be prone to becoming hysterical."

"Maybe she would benefit from fresh country air." Cherish wasn't going to miss an opportunity to hint about the farm.

Samuel held up his hands. "What do you call this air, stale?"

"I meant farm air."

Ada put her hand over her mouth and laughed. "Cherish, you'll never stop will you?"

Cherish sighed. "I just want to see the farm again to know that it's okay. It's hard trusting a stranger with the farm, my farm. I don't like to be a pest or annoy people all the time. I'd find the money and go there myself only I obviously can't stay at the house when he's there. We don't even have quarters where he could move to in the barn, but I could look at doing something like that. That could be a good idea and I can't believe that I only thought of it just now. It's a perfect solution." From Ada and Samuel's grim faces she knew they didn't agree with her.

"Just take no as a no," Samuel said.

Ada turned to her husband, tilting her head. "It's not a no. We said we'd take her in the warmer weather."

Samuel cleared his throat. "That's what I meant."

Ada wasn't letting him off the hook. "Then why didn't you say it?"

He rubbed his forehead. "Because I'm not as good at talking as you are, Dear."

Cherish looked back at the buggy and saw Bliss still in the driver's seat. "I guess I should go and see that she's okay. I'll get her home."

Ada stood up, leaned over and looked in Bliss's teacup. "She's hardly had any."

"Still, I should take her home."

"You only just got here," Ada said.

Samuel told his wife, "They probably have better things to do with their time today. Like be with people their own age." He smiled at Cherish. *"Denke* for coming here and delivering the news about tomorrow."

"Any time." Cherish stopped and thought about what she had said. "Oh, I hope I don't have any more news like that to give you in the future."

"I'm sure you won't." Samuel grinned.

"Can I take the things into the kitchen for you, Ada?" Cherish asked. She didn't want to get talked about once she left, because of not offering to help.

"Nee. I've got all day to do it. Now, I have all day tomorrow as well since I'm not going to your *haus* tomorrow afternoon for that important meeting. A meeting that will change lives and it will certainly have a big impact on Wilma herself and the rest of her *kinner.* It's not a decision that is to be made without a care."

Cherish nodded and wondered how Ada could've said so much without drawing a breath. "I agree. Well, goodbye, and *denke* for the tea and cookies." Cherish leaned over and grabbed another cookie. "I'll take one for Bliss if I might." Then she took another. "And, I might have another one myself."

Ada leaned forward and offered the plate to Cherish. "Why don't you take the whole thing?"

"*Nee.* Just the two will be fine."

"Bye, Cherish. It was nice to see you." There was a glint of amusement in Samuel's eyes.

"Bye again." Cherish was sure she'd said goodbye about six times. The whole interaction with them had been awkward and with Bliss running off like she'd done, everything had been left to her. Cherish walked down the porch steps nibbling on a cookie. It was so good.

Cherish finished hers by the time she reached the buggy. Then she passed

Bliss's through the window. "I got you a cookie."

"Oh, *denke.*"

Cherish leaned down and looked in the rear-view mirror of the buggy. Then she turned her head to both sides staring at her reflection. "Is there something wrong with my nose?"

"Nee. Why?"

"They said it was plain."

"Oh, I see what you mean. Ada said that something was as plain as the nose on your face. It means you can see it clearly, like you can see your nose because it's in the middle of your face."

Cherish gasped. "It's too big. That's what she meant!"

"She didn't mean *your* nose. Anyone's nose."

"I know, but still."

Bliss glanced over her shoulder. "Let's go, Cherish. They're looking at us."

Cherish had one last look at her nose before she unwrapped the reins from the post and climbed into the buggy. "Quick, let's go."

A giggle escaped Bliss's lips. "I'm sorry I started laughing. I feel so foolish now, but I couldn't stop."

"No need to feel bad. I'm sure they understood. I said you suffered from nerves."

As Bliss turned the horse down the driveway, she glanced down at the cookie. "Do you want the cookie? I'm not that hungry."

"Sure." Cherish wasted no time retrieving it from Bliss's lap.

"What did you say ... nerves?"

"*Jah.* I said, you had bad nerves."

"Oh, did you?"

Cherish swallowed her mouthful. "*Jah.* It seemed to make them happy. What else could I say?"

"I don't know. I was under so much pressure that I couldn't take it anymore. Is that 'nerves?' Ada is a little overbearing and that makes me want to laugh for some reason. I felt like I was somewhere else watching things as they play out. It makes me laugh more. Do you ever feel like that?"

"No, not at all. This cookie is so good, so crunchy yet it melts in your mouth. I think it's mostly sugar. They did say they'd take me to the farm."

"Oh, that's so good of them."

"Yeah, but when the weather's warmer. It'll probably never be warm enough for them. Old people feel the cold so much more than young people. I might as well give up."

"They meant it, Cherish. They said they'd do it and they're not going to say that and then not do it. And, they were the ones who wanted to sit outside, remember?"

Cherish sighed and looked out the window at the fields as she ate the last bite of the cookie. "I guess."

"Just be happy someone's going with you."

Cherish turned back to look at Bliss. "I could go by myself and stay with Ruth next door."

"*Jah,* but she's not in the community, is she?"

Cherish pouted. *"Nee,* but she's a good friend and was a good friend of Dagmar's too. Caroline's not in the community either and no one cares about that." Cherish sighed once more. "I haven't even asked *Mamm* if I can stay with Ruth. If I have to run away suddenly, that's my plan. I'll stay with Ruth until Malachi leaves the farm. Then I'll take over."

"Poor Malachi. Where would he go?"

"I don't know." Cherish shrugged her shoulders. "He's a grown man, it's not my problem. He knows he's not there forever. I told him that from the get-go." Cherish saw the concern on Bliss's face. "The problem with you is you're too sensitive."

"Do you think so?"

"Not everyone has feelings like you. People don't care so much about things. Take Malachi for example, he'll just be happy to be on his way so he can get something more steady. He might be one of those men who never want to settle anywhere permanent. He might like to be a few years here and a few years there."

"Where?"

"I don't know. Here and there."

"I'll come visit you on the farm. I'll miss you when you leave for good."

Cherish liked the sound of that. She had hoped that Favor would come with her or at least visit often. Now Favor was too caught up with Caroline. Caroline had stolen Favor away from her. She was a sister thief. Cherish had to make do with Bliss, but that wasn't so bad. "I'll have a bedroom just for you. I'll make it real pretty."

Bliss glanced at her, taking her eyes from the road for a moment. "Would you really keep a bedroom just for me?"

"Sure. You're the best stepsister I ever had."

Bliss smiled and then looked over at Cherish. "What about Florence?"

"She's my half-sister."

"Oh, yes, of course she is." Bliss shook her head. "It all gets a little confusing sometimes. But that makes me your only stepsister."

"I guess it does, but if I had more, you'd still be the best and most favorite."

"*Denke,* Cherish. That makes me so happy."

"Do we have to go straight home?" Cherish asked.

"I don't think so. They didn't say to come back right away, did they?"

"*Nee*. Not that I remember, but I wasn't listening."

"Where do you want to go?" Bliss asked.

"Let's visit Joy and Isaac, see how they're coming along with the repairs to the house."

"Okay. Oh, but we didn't bring anything. Should we go back home and get some cookies or something?"

Cherish put her hand over her stomach. She'd overdone it a little with Ada's cookies. "*Nee*. She'll just be happy to see us."

Chapter 4

When they were outside Joy's house, they saw from the horse and buggy outside that Joy and Isaac already had visitors.

"I think that buggy belongs to the Millers," Bliss said. "That'll be Hope and Fairfax visiting them."

"No. I know all their horses and I don't think it's one of theirs. It might be someone else. Let's not interrupt them."

"You're right. Anyway, since we're talking about Hope, she didn't look too happy today and she wouldn't tell me what was wrong. It might be nothing, but still ..."

Cherish's mouth fell open when she thought about Hope telling Bliss things and not telling her. "You think Hope might be in there right now telling Joy some secrets?"

"Maybe."

Cherish frowned. "Secrets about what?"

"About why she hasn't been herself lately. I just know something's going on."

"*Nee*, because it's not Fairfax and Hope. Don't you ever listen when I talk? I said it's not one of the Millers' horses."

Bliss shrugged, and signaled Charlie to move.

Cherish turned around and watched the cottage get smaller, hoping someone would come out and wave for them to come back. No one did, so Cherish faced the front. "Why aren't you with Adam today?"

"He wanted to spend the day sleeping. He works so hard. He's coming for dinner tonight."

"Fair enough. Everyone works hard, don't they."

"Some more than others."

With her fingertips Cherish brushed the cookie crumbs off the woolen blanket. "If I had a boyfriend, I wouldn't be so bored all the time. I could be out with him right now."

"I thought you said you liked the reporter. What's his name again?"

"Daniel Withers. I do like him, but it's odd with him being an *Englisher*. I don't know if he likes me. He told me to call him and I feel like I'm calling him all the time. He made some excuse about why he couldn't call me."

"It might not be an excuse. *Mamm* and Levi wouldn't be happy if they knew Daniel liked you or the other way around."

"Yeah, well, Florence married an *Englisher* and that turned out well. Anyway, I'm putting Daniel on a shelf right now and forgetting about him."

"A shelf?"

"*Jah,* a shelf in my head. Now stop talking about him. I know you're changing the subject because you don't want to tell me about Adam." Cherish poked Bliss in the ribs causing her to giggle.

"I'm not doing that. I'd tell you about him, but there's nothing to tell."

"Okay. I'll tell you what I've been thinking about Daniel. When we see each other, all seems good, but he doesn't adore me. I want someone who adores me like Adam adores you. He came here to be with you. Daniel can't even pick up a phone, or make any effort at all."

A smile spread over Bliss's face. "I like the sound of that. Do you think Adam adores me?"

"You know he does. He moved away from all his friends and family to be close to you. You'll be married in a few years. Maybe a year or two and … I better make that bedroom in my house a room for two because you'll be married by the time I get there." Cherish laughed. "I can't wait to make the place feel like my own with new curtains and everything. I'll paint all the furniture blue. Blue's my favorite color right now. Everything will be blue. I'll leave the floorboards."

"Will the farm produce enough income to keep it going? From what you said, Malachi has been doing some juggling to make a living. Would you get time for making things?"

"Of course. If someone else can do it. I can do it. Dagmar had time to make baskets and all kinds of things."

"Okay. You're right. It is nice to have someone. I'm not so lonely now since *Dat* married your *mamm*. I've got so many sisters now, and none of you treat me any different."

"You are one of us." Cherish huffed. "Now you've got me thinking. It's Sunday, what would Daniel Withers be doing and why hasn't he called me? I don't even know where he lives. He told me to call him, but I'm not going to be a man chaser. He's the man, he should chase me if he's interested. He seems to be when we're together. I can't work it out."

"Maybe you should forget him. Leave him on that shelf. I don't think he'll join us like Fairfax did and you thinking about him too much is not good. I shouldn't have mentioned him. What happened to Caroline? Didn't she like him too?"

"He's fallen to second in line. She's set her eyes on Eddie, the beekeeper."

"Eddie? He's nice and all but he doesn't seem her type. He's a little too plain or something."

Cherish didn't like the sound of that. She'd gone to a lot of trouble to have Caroline like Eddie, and she'd even schooled Eddie on how to make Caroline like him. She'd have to stop by and check on his progress. Caroline had not mentioned Eddie lately. What if things had ground to a halt? "Don't tell her you think he's not suited, whatever you do."

"Nee. I won't give her my opinion. Unless she asks for it, but she probably won't. She hardly talks to me. I haven't heard her talk about him. He's quiet and she's not quiet."

"That could be the attraction. You know what they say about opposites."

"I don't."

"Opposites attract."

"I just can't see her with Eddie." Bliss shook her head. "And like I said, she hasn't even talked about him."

"That is odd, but you're right. I've been tardy, I've let things slide without following through. I'll have to see about that."

"Don't meddle, Cherish."

"Meddle? What's that?" Cherish knew very well what it was to meddle.

"Getting involved in people's lives and making things happen to put them together, or tear them apart like what you did with that letter to Adam."

"You should be thanking me for that. It's because of me that he came back to enable you to pinch him from me."

Bliss pressed her lips together and shook her head. "I'm not so sure about that since I didn't even know about it at the time. It might have turned out differently. Besides, if *Gott* wanted us to be together, He would've found a way. There could've been many ways we would've found each other again."

"I said I was sorry about the letter. I didn't think you'd keep bringing it up or I wouldn't have apologized the first time around. He probably knew the letter was from me anyway and he came back to see you as an excuse. It was also an excuse to get me into trouble." Cherish pushed her lips into a pout.

"You don't need anyone's help to get into trouble."

"I've changed. It would help if everyone stopped bringing up what I did in the past. It will drag me back down to where I once was."

"Okay. I'm sorry."

"Good." Cherish smiled at Bliss. "I forgive you."

"That's good of you."

Cherish frowned at Bliss wondering if she was being sarcastic. She wasn't sure. "Well, where should we go and what should we do today?"

"Maybe go home? I want to spend time with *Dat* and *Mamm*."

Cherish slumped down further in the buggy seat. How was that even possible? How boring it would be to sit and spend time with that boring couple. Besides, they saw them every day, why add to that? "They're home every single day and mostly so are we."

"I know, but we're always doing chores or working in the shop. There's no time to just sit and talk."

"There is, at night."

"We're always outside talking with Caroline."

"Hmm. I'm not sure why. Why should we talk with her? Maybe we're enabling her smoking habit. If we stayed inside, she probably wouldn't smoke as much if she was alone."

"I like her."

Cherish rolled her eyes. What was there to like about Caroline? Cherish thought of what else they could do, or maybe there was someone else to visit. "Florence. We could visit her and play with Iris."

"Okay. I'd love that."

Chapter 5

Florence sat with Carter in the living room in front of the fire as they drank coffee. Their minds were on their meeting with Levi and Wilma the next day. Levi had told them he had some ideas to put forward and it was no secret that they all wanted to get something final decided so they could move on with their lives. Florence had told them she wouldn't take over the ownership of the orchard and to leave things be, but Levi wasn't happy with that knowing Wilma had hidden the will that stated Florence had inherited the Baker Apple Orchard when Florence's father—Wilma's first husband—had died.

"I hope we can resolve this once and for all tomorrow," Carter said. "It's been so much like a chess game."

Florence laughed. "You think the world is one large chess game."

"If you knew more about the game, you'd agree with me. We're moving in on the king and he's going to surrender."

"Oh that's awful. Are you saying Levi is the king? We're not forcing anyone to do anything." Florence reached for her mug of coffee.

"We have made moves."

"Not calculated ones." After Florence sipped her drink, she warmed her hands around the mug.

Carter smiled and shook his finger at her. "Moves are moves, no matter what the intention is behind them. We make a move, as in we do or say something, then we wait for the other person's reaction, which is their move."

"All I want now is for the orchard to do well and for the trees and soil to remain healthy. I told them to leave things be, but Levi is insisting to include me. So is that his move?"

Carter leaned back. "Hmm. Sounds like he might have skipped his turn, allowing you to get ahead. Anyway, chess aside, do you think he wants you included because of pride?"

"I don't think so, not pride in a bad sense. He'd see me not taking some form of ownership over the orchard as him getting a handout maybe. Or me doing him a favor, which would probably be the same thing in his eyes. I think he'd have been horribly embarrassed by Wilma hiding *Dat's* will. I don't know how it's all going to work out. Do you have any ideas you can add to the discussion?"

"I haven't thought too much about it. I think it's got to come from them. The only thing that needs to be worked out is that you need to be in charge of the place if it's ever going to turn around and make a decent profit. It's no secret the Baker Apple Orchard has taken a drastic downturn since you left. Everyone admits that now."

"I know. I think they can see it."

"It'll take a lot for Levi to put you in charge. Number one, you're a woman, and number two, wouldn't that mean that you are in charge of him? Isn't the man supposed to be the head?" Carter took his mug off the coffee table.

"I know what you're saying, but this situation is a little different. Besides, when he thought the orchard was Wilma's he didn't mind that."

"That's true, but from what you said he was still calling the shots."

"That would've been okay because Wilma is the kind of person who prefers to take a backseat. She said he wanted to try his hand at running an orchard so she allowed him. Wilma doesn't know the first thing about the orchard. She's never been hands on. Even at harvests, she prepared food for the workers and never was involved in the collection of apples or even the sorting. Levi had no choice but to manage it all even if he'd been reluctant to do so. Sell it or manage it himself, those would have been the only two options he would've seen."

"It might come as a relief for him to hand that side of things over to you."

"That's what I'm thinking especially after his heart attack."

They both jumped in fright when someone banged loudly on their door. Spot leaped from the couch and ran to the door, barking.

"I wonder who that is?" Carter got to his feet, and then they heard Iris crying. Carter said over his shoulder, as he headed to the door. "It's got to be one of your bonnet sisters. No one else would knock that loudly."

Florence knew he was right. "They've woken the baby. I was hoping for another half hour at least." They'd set aside the time to discuss tomorrow's meeting, and now they'd been interrupted. "I'll get Iris."

While Florence was walking up the stairs to the nursery, Carter opened the door to see it wasn't just one bonnet sister, it was two. "Good morning," he said with a grin. "Come in."

Cherish walked in ahead of Bliss. "Iris is awake. I heard her. Can I see her please, please, please?" She walked a few more steps and then spun around before Bliss even had a chance to move.

Once Bliss was inside, he closed the door. "She is awake *now*. Florence will bring her down. Have a seat."

Just as they sat down, Florence walked down the stairs with the baby.

Cherish jumped up. "Oh, look at her in that pink dress. I want a pink dress now. A matching one. Ah, she looks adorable. Can I have a hold?" She reached out her arms for the baby.

"Hello, Cherish," Florence said.

Cherish laughed. "Oh, I'm being rude. Hello, Florence. Everything goes out of my head when I see Iris. I get totally focused on her. I can't believe how big she's getting. She'll be walking and talking soon."

Florence handed the baby over, and then looked over at Bliss. "Morning, Bliss."

"Good morning, Florence. I hope you two don't mind us stopping by like this."

"Of course not. You can come here any time you like," Carter told her.

Cherish sat carefully and then sniffed Iris. "She's not due for a diaper change, is she?"

"She's dry. I checked."

When Iris started squirming and moving her arms about, Carter told Cherish, "She likes to be upright."

Cherish placed her over her shoulder. "Like this?"

"Yes. Just like that."

Cherish stood and rocked Iris to and fro while patting her back.

Florence sat down next to Carter. "I haven't seen Joy for a while. She must be getting bigger."

"She is. She's only got two and a half months to go. I can't wait for their baby to be born. I'm hoping it's a girl."

"*Dat* said you're both coming tomorrow night to talk about the orchard," Bliss said.

"To make a decision about the orchard," Cherish corrected her.

"We are," Florence said, "but it's in the afternoon. At three. I'll be glad when something's finalized."

"Who's looking after Iris?" Cherish asked. "Because I could come here and watch her while you're there."

"So could I. Me too," Bliss blurted out. "We could both do it. Or you could bring her with you. *Jah,* of course you'd do that."

Carter kept turning his head from side to side looking at whoever was speaking.

"I've asked Christina to mind her while we're there. We're taking Iris to her place."

Cherish pouted. "We could've done it."

"Next time, maybe," said Florence, plumping up a cushion behind her. "So what have you two got planned for the day?"

"I'll probably go home and write letters after Cherish and I watch Cottonball play in her enclosure. And then Adam is coming for dinner. Also, Ada and Samuel are visiting later today too. We just visited them because *Mamm* invited them for the meeting you're having tomorrow and *Dat* wasn't happy about that."

"We had to uninvite them," explained Cherish.

Florence made a face. "Oh, that would've been awkward."

"It was. Ada hit us with one hundred and ten questions. She was upset and said *Mamm* would've wanted her there to have her opinion."

Bliss added, "Seems *Dat* doesn't care for their opinion. He said the orchard's nothing to do with them."

Cherish looked at Florence. "Are you glad they're not coming?"

Florence knew she had to be careful how she answered. Things were so often repeated and sounded far worse than they were. "I'm always happy to see them, but I can see Levi's point of view. He wants to work things out between the four of us."

Iris whimpered and turned her head. "Ah, she's looking for her *mamm,*" Cherish said.

"Can I have a hold first before you give her back, Cherish?"

"Sure." Cherish walked over with Iris and handed her to Bliss.

Bliss stared at the baby in her arms. "She's so beautiful."

"We think so," said Carter, smiling.

"When will you have another baby?" Cherish asked. "I can't have too many nephews and nieces, especially if I'm going to sit on the fence like Aunt Dagmar."

Carter burst out laughing. "I think you mean on the shelf, Cherish. You'll be left on the shelf if you don't get married. That was the olden day view of things. Sitting on the fence is where you don't want to make a decision."

"What I said was right," Cherish said. "I'll sit on the fence until I make a decision to get married."

Carter shook his head, keeping quiet.

Florence breathed out heavily. "We do want a second child and possibly a third, but there are so many things around here …"

Carter added, "We've got to build the new house first. The plans are complete and they'll start digging the foundations soon.

Once we have our new home, then we'll have more." He smiled at Florence.

Cherish noticed the love they shared and decided she wanted that one day for herself. But did the perfect man exist? She wouldn't settle for less. Daniel wasn't perfect because he wasn't chasing her. Besides, he was an *Englisher.* At one time, she had thought Adam Wengerd might've been the one, but he only had eyes for Bliss.

"She's not crying now that I'm holding her," Bliss said.

Cherish frowned at the way Iris was sitting on Bliss's lap only supported by one hand around her back. "She wasn't crying before. She was just making noises. And be careful she doesn't make any sudden movements. You might drop her."

"I won't, Cherish. I'm holding her good enough. I didn't say that to you when you were holding her."

"I'm watching. She's doing fine," Carter said.

Cherish ignored Carter, and kept speaking to Bliss. "Just use both hands, would you? She's my niece. I don't want her to fall."

"Well, she's kind of like mine too and I wouldn't want her to fall either. I wouldn't want any baby to fall." Bliss looked at Florence. "Isn't she my niece too?"

"Of course she is, Bliss."

"Yeah, she'll call you Step Aunt Bliss when she can talk. I'll be Favorite Aunt Cherish. That's what she'll call me."

Florence frowned at Cherish. "No, Cherish. Iris will call her Aunt Bliss."

"I was only joking, Florence. I wasn't serious."

"Be careful what you say. Even in jokes, people can get hurt," Florence told Cherish.

"It did upset me," Bliss said in a small voice. "I know you didn't mean it, but still …"

"See, Florence? She knew I didn't mean—"

"That's not the point I'm trying to make." Florence frowned at Cherish.

Carter bounded to his feet. "Shall I make us some hot chocolate?"

"Yes please." Cherish smiled at him.

"Me too," added Bliss.

"Florence?" Carter asked.

"I'll have a cup too, thanks." Florence had to smile. Carter was uncomfortable when the girls bickered. She probably could've stopped it going further, but Cherish had to be corrected when she was out of line. Carter had made an extra effort with them, she'd noticed. She wondered how he'd be when Iris grew older and had siblings. Hopefully, they wouldn't be as bad.

"Oh look! She can sit up by herself," Cherish said pointing at Iris.

"I'm supporting her and ready to catch her if she falls, but she is holding herself upright and strong," Bliss said.

Florence laughed. "I know. She'll be walking in no time. She's growing up too fast for my liking."

Chapter 6

A few hours earlier.

Hope couldn't stop smiling when she looked out the window and saw Fairfax's borrowed horse and buggy approach the house. He didn't have his own horse or buggy, and the Millers had been letting him use one of their horses and the spare buggy. When he left the dairy, he'd need to get his own.

Hope ran down the stairs to see him. "Bye, *Mamm,* bye Levi."

"Wait. Where are you going?" *Mamm* asked.

"Out with Fairfax." Then Hope stopped still. "Can he come for dinner tonight?"

Mamm smiled. "Of course he can. Adam will be here too."

Hope hurried out the door, yelling a thank you over her shoulder. She stopped on the porch expecting him to be out front, but he wasn't. She looked down the driveway to see that he'd stopped to talk to Favor and Caroline. They were standing near the buggy on the driver's side talking to him.

Stepping down from the porch, her eyes were fixed only on Caroline.

Was there any truth to what Cherish was constantly telling her?

Did Caroline have a crush on Fairfax?

He'd made a commitment to the Amish community and to her—Hope. His commitment to her, though, was a private one and there was nothing to stop him going back on it.

After all, it wasn't a sin to change one's mind.

Hope wouldn't feel truly secure until a wedding date was announced. It didn't matter how far away that date was as long as the final commitment was made. She couldn't even begin to think how awful her life would be without him.

When she stood waiting in open view, Fairfax looked up and waved. He then said something to the girls and they moved away allowing him to move his horse and buggy to meet her.

When he drew level with her, he stopped and she climbed up next to him.

"You look lovely today, Hope."

She didn't feel lovely.

Inside, she was rumbling with insecurity.

She couldn't be a pushy woman and question him about what he was doing and ask why he hadn't made plans. That was not the kind of person she was. She forced a smile at his comment about looking lovely. "I do?"

"You always look lovely." He reached for her hand and gave it a squeeze. Then he moved the buggy closer to the house so he could turn it around.

Once they were heading down the driveway, Hope looked around for Favor and Caroline. "Where are the girls?"

"In the shop. That's where they came out of."

"That's weird for them to be in there on a Sunday."

"Maybe they're using that as their private retreat away from others."

"What did they say to you?"

He hesitated while he moved onto the road, then he glanced over at her. "Just general chit chat."

"Like what?"

"They asked what we were doing today and that kind of thing."

She laughed but it came out as more of a grumble. "I don't even know what we're doing today. Funny that they should find out before me."

Fairfax frowned and didn't even look over at her. "We're just taking time to be alone. I don't care where we do that."

"Well, what did you tell them?"

He shrugged. "I can't remember."

"It was only two seconds ago."

When he pinched his eyebrows together, she realized how awful she sounded. Like a probing octopus with tentacles reaching into his brain. She didn't want to drive him away.

Part of her just wanted to come right out and tell him what had been bothering her, but then she'd be annoyed that she had to.

She didn't want to force him to do things. That was not the kind of relationship she wanted. A good relationship should flow, each doing what the other wanted without knowing it. At least, that's how she thought one should be.

"You okay?" He glanced at her again.

"*Jah*, just fine."

"Truly?"

She shrugged her shoulders. "Everyone's on edge today because there's a meeting with Florence and Carter about the orchard tomorrow. They're finally going to make something official about the orchard."

"Good. It's about time. It feels like it's been dragging on forever."

"I know and it's awful when things drag on forever, isn't it?" She looked at him, hoping he'd get her point, but he made no comment. So she went even further. "Poor Florence would've been just hanging around not knowing about the future. I think everyone needs to know what their future holds, don't you?"

"It would be good, but sometimes that's not possible. Look at Levi. No one could've foreseen he'd have that heart attack. He could've died."

"I know. That's true, but good thing he didn't."

"*Jah.*"

"Florence is a lot like me, she wants to know where she's going in a few years' time and what she'll be doing."

"Now you've got me thinking."

Hope was delighted that her words had worked on him. "I have?"

"Yes. I'm thinking tomorrow's meeting might present me with an opportunity to work where I've wanted to work all along. Back in an orchard."

"Oh. Then you'd leave the Millers?" She hoped he'd talk about where 'they'd' live. In the past, he'd always said they'd get married as soon as possible. Now he had finished the instructions, got baptized, so what was stopping them?

"Jah, I'd have to leave them but they shouldn't have any problem replacing me with another worker."

Hope scratched her neck.

"Where are we going?" he asked when he came to a T intersection.

"Take a left here. So, you're thinking if Florence takes over the orchard then she'd have three in a row and then there'd be work for you?"

"Exactly. I'm sure they could use an extra worker."

She really wanted to ask where 'he'd' live, but if he gave her an answer rather than talk about where 'they'd' live, she'd probably burst into tears. "I think you're right. You will get a job with them whichever way it goes tomorrow. I mean, we've lost Honor and Mercy when they got married, and Bliss will marry Adam one day soon, I'd think. Joy's married now, so she's not working there, either."

"Caroline said she's been helping out a lot," Fairfax said.

"She's not much help. She's talking about doing other things anyway."

"What kind of things?"

"I'm surprised you haven't heard."

"I haven't heard a thing."

"She wants to arrange tours to the bee place over behind our property."

"The B Right Honey Company?"

"That's right."

He laughed. "What does Eddie say about that?"

"He said he's talking to his father, but that was several weeks ago. I'm not sure what came of that. Then she wants people to pay for going on a tour of the Baker Apple Orchard. Come to think of it, she hasn't mentioned either of those things for weeks."

"I can see it would work."

"I don't know. There's a lot that would have to go into it. And we'd need to get the orchard back on track first. I think Caroline would be back at her own home by the time that happens."

"She's been here a while."

"It was only meant to be a week or so."

"Hope, I haven't been truthful about something and I'm hoping you'll forgive me."

Her heart pounded and she held her breath thinking she'd pass out. If there was one thing she would not tolerate in a husband, it was being lied to. "What is it?"

"I've made plans."

A smile spread across her face. Wedding plans! He had finally made marriage plans. She'd been worried for nothing. "You have?"

"Yes, and Mrs. Miller kindly packed you and me a picnic lunch." He looked over and gave her a big smile.

She waited for more, but nothing more came. When it sunk in that his 'plans' involved a picnic, Hope covered her face with her hands, smiling. As tragic as it was, she saw the funny side. "Ah, it was so sweet of her to do that."

"I know. She's my Amish *Mamm,* and she really likes you."

Hope felt better knowing that she had Mrs. Miller's approval, and that it seemed to mean a lot to Fairfax. After all, she knew Mrs. Miller wouldn't approve of Caroline. She wasn't even in their community. "I think we're going to have a really good afternoon."

"I always have a good time when I'm with you. Now, let's find a good place for a picnic, and not a paddock somewhere. It might have a bull in it."

Hope laughed. "And you'd know the difference now since you spend all your day with cows."

"Hey, I knew the difference before that. Remember that I'm not a city boy."

Hope laughed and felt a little better, but it would take a marriage date to take away her anxiety. There was a small fearful voice in her mind that kept telling her Fairfax would change his mind; it was silently eating away at her.

Chapter 7

"It's so nice of you to do this. You always make me feel special," Hope told Fairfax.

"I try to. I'd do more if I wasn't so busy all the time. Even when it's Sunday we still have to milk the cows."

"I know that."

He unfolded the checkered blanket and swooshed it through the air and gently spread it on the ground. The cool wind quickly tilted up the corners, so Hope promptly sat down. "I hope this breeze dies down soon."

"Aw, don't let it bother you. We're here and we are alone. That's rare, so we should enjoy it. I'm surprised one of your sisters didn't want to come with us."

"They were all off doing other things."

"Good for us!" He knelt down and made to open the picnic hamper but she put her hand on his. "Let me do it. It's a woman's job to look after her man."

He laughed. "If you say so. I like the sound of that." He sat down, putting his legs straight out in front of him. She opened the lid and passed him a hand-hemmed fabric napkin.

"One for you and one for me." She tossed hers down on the other side where she'd been sitting. "Now, let's see what goodies your Amish *Mamm* has put in here for us today. I think I smell some fried chicken." She pulled out a bottle of cider. "Oh, I hope she got this from our store." She had a better look at the pale green glass and also the screw top. "I think it is one of our bottles."

"She said it came from your shop. She always buys your products, just like you get your milk from her."

"Good. I'll have to bring her some bottles soon and leave them with her and maybe some apple pies. It's the least we can do for her since she's been looking after you so well."

"She'd love that."

Hope passed him the bottle and two glasses. "You pour."

"Yes, Ma'am."

"It's *jah*. You really should start using the Pennsylvania Dutch I've been teaching you."

"I do know a lot. I don't know why I don't use it. *Jah, meine fraa.*"

She giggled. "That's right. Get used to saying that. Don't forget it." She hoped he'd talk more about her becoming his *fraa,* but too quickly the conversation went in a different direction and their time together flew by.

As soon as Fairfax drove Hope back to the house, he headed off to join the Millers' for the afternoon milking.

When Hope walked through the front door of her home, Cherish ran out from the kitchen and grabbed her wrist. "Hope, come here." Cherish dragged her through the house and straight out the back door.

When Cherish closed the door and folded her arms, glaring at her, Hope thought something bad had happened. "What's wrong?"

Cherish pursed her lips. "I don't know. You tell me."

Hope looked at Cherish. "What's going on?"

"I can tell something's not right with you. Do you have a secret?" She put her arms by her side. "Or has something happened between you and Fairfax?"

"Don't be silly."

"I'm not. Tell me."

Hope sighed and her shoulders lowered. "We did have a nice day," she said in a small voice.

"But?" Cherish asked. "If you have a secret or a problem, you need to share it before it becomes a burden. That's what happens, I'm told." Then she noticed Hope was having trouble looking her in the eyes. "I'm sensing you wanted to say, "But ..." So, what is the but? You had a nice day, but ... what?"

"But he always said that we'd marry as soon as he became a member of the community. Am I married yet?"

"No, but you will be."

"When?"

Cherish was pleased she'd been right. It wasn't exactly a secret, but it was something. "Have you talked about that with him?"

"No. I couldn't. I don't want to be pushy."

Cherish couldn't quite understand why her sister had a problem with saying what she wanted. "It's not pushy to tell him how you're feeling."

"I want Fairfax to be the one to talk about it. If he really loved me, he wouldn't be able to wait to marry me. I spent the whole day with him, well, half a day and he didn't mention marriage once. When he'd first made the decision to join us, he was talking about it all the time. It just scares me."

"Scares you?"

"He could change his mind or meet someone else."

"No. He loves you."

"I feel that he does, but then why isn't he doing something about it?"

Cherish bit her lip. She had no answer. "He's waiting for everything to be perfect."

"Or, is he waiting for me to be perfect? Is there something about me that's not perfect for him?"

"You are perfect."

Hope smiled. *"Denke,* Cherish. It's nice of you to say, but does he think that?"

"He should. If he has any sense. Don't worry, it'll work out."

"I do worry. Do you see why I'm a little nervous?"

Cherish knew exactly how Hope felt. "You're worried about nothing. Everything will fall into place soon. He sees you every spare moment he has. And he's coming for dinner tonight, isn't he?"

"Girls."

They both looked around at *Mamm.*

"We need the vegetables peeled and the peas shelled."

"Coming, *Mamm.*"

They walked into the house together and sat at the kitchen table in front of a heap of vegetables. Cherish started on the carrots, while Hope chose to shell the peas. As soon as *Mamm* left the kitchen, their conversation resumed.

"What were you saying before, Cherish?" Hope popped a pea into her mouth.

"I said Fairfax is coming for the evening meal and he sees you every chance he has, so there's no need to worry. What if someone brings marriage up in conversation while we're eating? I could say something about you two getting married and see what he says."

Hope swallowed the pea. "Don't you dare. That would be dreadful. Please don't, and don't get anyone else to do that either."

"Okay, it was just an idea."

"*Nee.*" Hope shook her head. "I'll just need to have patience and trust in *Gott* that everything will be fine."

"It will be fine. In my heart, I know it. You two are perfect together. You're like the most perfect couple. You're just as perfect as Florence and Carter."

"Do you think so?"

"I do. Fairfax is so nice. Everyone likes him."

"I know. That is another cause for concern. It could be another problem."

"Aww. Don't start worrying about silly things. Aunt Dagmar used to say most of the things we worry about never ever happen."

"That's true. I'll try not to."

"Aunt Dagmar used to say don't try, just—"

"I know, she said just to do it."

"Oh, have I mentioned that before?"

"Once or twice. Don't forget ..." Hope put her finger to her mouth. "Not a word when he comes here tonight."

"You already said that. I told you I'd keep quiet."

"Good."

"You had a good day?" Cherish asked.

"I did. We had a picnic in a field. It wasn't a nice field, but it didn't matter."

Cherish frowned. "You mean, you didn't visit Joy and Isaac earlier?"

"No."

"Oh. Bliss and I drove past and we thought we saw the Millers' horse and buggy. It must've been someone else's." So, Cherish thought, she had been right about the horse.

"It wasn't us."

"Do you have something else you want to share with me, hmmm?"

Hope smiled. "Definitely not."

When they heard their mother walking back into the kitchen, Cherish whispered to Hope, "It must be so nice to be in love."

"It was. I mean, it is."

Chapter 8

That night over dinner, Cherish had a hard time keeping her mouth closed.

She kept a close eye on Hope and a close eye on Fairfax, and noticed something. Every now and again, Hope's gaze traveled to Caroline. So then, Cherish shifted her focus to their *English* visitor, Caroline. Hope was concerned over Caroline's interest in Fairfax.

By the time the main course was over, Cherish concluded that Caroline spent far too much time looking across the table at both Fairfax and Adam. It frustrated her. Couldn't her mother and Levi see that Caroline should be sent home as quick as possible? It wasn't normal to keep her here for so long. No other family in the community had English visitors stay for that length of time.

When the vegetable bowls and meat platters had been cleared off the center of the table and replaced with fruit salad, ice-cream and raspberry tart, Cherish was first to offer the bowls around.

"Caroline, how's your house coming along? Is it rebuilt yet?" Cherish asked, making sure she smiled sweetly.

Caroline glared at her. They both knew it had been a lie when Caroline had told Wilma and Levi that her family's house burned down right after Levi hinted that she go home. "It's not far off from completion, but they've had to order a special roof tile and the order is coming from overseas." She twisted a long golden spiral of hair around her finger, without taking her eyes off Cherish.

"Why's that?" Levi asked.

She smiled at Levi. "I'm not sure. I guess they're rebuilding it how they always dreamed of having a home. After all, their insurance is paying for it."

"That's convenient," Levi said.

"I know. They're happy about it. Not so happy about having nowhere to stay. They're going from one friend's place to another."

"They'll be glad to finally get back into their own home again," Wilma said.

"And I'm sure you can't wait to see your new home too," Cherish added.

"That's right." Caroline then looked down at her food and helped herself to a spoonful of ice cream.

Levi said, "We're having a meeting tomorrow with Florence and Carter. We're sorting things out for good. Tomorrow a final decision on the orchard will be made. I just thought you should all know that."

Adam grinned. "Ah, that's a hint for us that we're not to come for the evening meal tomorrow night, is it?"

Levi's eyes twinkled with mischief. "It wasn't a hint. More of a warning."

"Levi doesn't mean it's a warning. Everything will go fine. We all want the same thing, the four of us," Wilma said.

Cherish was disturbed by her mother's comment. She could afford to be adult about it now and be onboard with trying to work things out, but she was the direct cause of so many of the upsets in their family. For a while Cherish had felt bad about exposing *Mamm's* error in judgement about keeping *Dat's* will hidden, but now she was glad she had done it.

She'd had to, otherwise, she'd be just as bad as her mother. The only thing she regretted was snooping through her mother's things. She'd had no bad intentions. She'd been looking for some kind of document revealing who actually owned the orchard since Levi had kept referring to it as his. She hadn't been expecting to find what she had found.

Cherish stared at Levi while he carefully spooned some cut fruit into his bowl. Did he feel the same about Wilma as before, now that he knew she was dishonest?

It scared Cherish a little that a person could marry someone and not really know them. She had to be sure she didn't make that same error. "Ada and Samuel said they were going to come here today and they didn't, did they?" Cherish asked.

"*Nee*, they didn't," Wilma said. "I hope they're not upset about you uninviting them."

"Me?" Cherish's mouth dropped open. "We didn't, you did. We were just delivering the message."

"Beware delivering bad news to people," Levi said. "When David heard that Jonathan and Saul were dead, David slew the messenger who brought the news."

Cherish's mouth dropped open. "You could've told me that yesterday. You were sending me into the lions' den."

"That was a different story," Bliss said, smiling.

Wilma looked down. "Maybe Ada and Samuel are upset with me."

Cherish nodded. *"Jah,* that would make sense. No point killing the messenger."

Hope, who was sitting next to Cherish, dug her in the ribs.

"Well, it doesn't make sense. It's not the messenger's fault."

Levi looked at Bliss. "You explained the situation to them, didn't you?"

"Jah. We told them what was happening and they were fine with it. They seemed fine with it."

Cherish didn't like to say anything, but didn't Bliss notice how upset Ada had been? Cherish looked from Bliss to her mother.

Were Ada and her mother going to have a falling out over this?

They'd been best friends for years.

Maybe Ada should've been told it was Levi's decision not to have them there, but then she would've been upset with Levi. And, Ada was the type of woman to say something to him.

"This has been a *wunderbaar* meal," Adam said.

"*Denke,* Adam." Wilma smiled at him. "All the girls helped."

"Including me," Caroline giggled, causing Cherish to roll her eyes. She'd helped with the meatloaf yesterday and part of the meal they had eaten included the leftovers. She'd not lifted a finger over the preparation of tonight's meal.

Cherish stifled her annoyance and looked at Hope. She looked so sad that Cherish knew she had to do something about it. If Fairfax had lost interest in Hope, or changed his mind, she had to help. She couldn't sit back and do nothing and leave Hope feeling miserable, wondering why he was taking his time.

That night, Hope didn't go outside with the girls when their visitors went home. She sat down with her mother instead and watched her knit Joy's soon-to-be-born baby a fine white woolen shawl.

Wilma looked up at her. "Where's your knitting?"

"Oh, that was just a blanket I started for Joy's *boppli*. It looked awful. It's up in my room."

"Go fetch it. I'll help you with it."

"Maybe later. I'm not in the mood. It'll have to be unraveled and started over. I might do that tomorrow night."

"Suit yourself."

"I'm happy to sit here and watch you knit. Your fingers move so fast. I wish mine were that quick."

"They will be in thirty or forty more years if you do as much knitting as I've done."

"I hope so. I guess I won't be fast if I don't do the practice." Hope sat on her fingers to keep them warm.

"That's for certain." Wilma chuckled. "I can't wait until Joy has her *boppli*. It'll be my fourth *grosskin*."

"I know."

"What is wrong with Mercy and Honor? They should both be pregnant again by now."

"They will be soon, I guess."

"I thought they'd be like me. I had the six of you girls one after the other with hardly any space in between. You're all a year apart."

When *Mamm* looked over at her, Hope forced a smile. She didn't want her mother to know how depressed she was. All this talk about babies wasn't helping either. She'd always wanted a baby quickly after she married, so she'd feel complete with a family. But now, even that was moving further away. At this rate, Cherish would be married before her.

Mamm got to the end of the row and looked around. "Levi's having an early night again, and I normally sit up alone. Why aren't you out with the others?"

"It's too cold for that. Are you happy now things ... how things have turned out with the orchard?"

Wilma frowned at her. "I hope I will be when we finalize everything tomorrow."

"Oh that's right."

"Is everything all right with you, Hope? Levi told everyone over the meal that we're meeting with them tomorrow. Didn't you hear him?"

"*Jah.* It's all good. I was just thinking about something else."

"Well ... what is it? Secrets don't do anyone any good. I found that out the hard way. If you have a problem you should tell me. I am your *mudder,* after all."

Hope smiled. "I know you are." It wouldn't do any good to tell anyone else. The last thing she needed was someone else talking to Fairfax. It could drive him away completely. "I just need a good sleep. I haven't been able to sleep lately and I don't know why." Hope slumped back into the chair and tucked her legs under her.

"Why don't you move bedrooms to the one next to the chimney? It's a warmer room. Sometimes I can't sleep if I'm too cold."

"I won't move bedrooms, but I will take another blanket."

"*Jah*. We've plenty." Wilma sighed. "I would love to visit Mercy and Honor again, but it's difficult to get away from here. So much is going on."

"I know. Maybe they'll visit us in the summertime."

"Possibly. I can only hope and pray that they will."

"Can I do a few rows, *Mamm?*" Hope asked.

Wilma stopped knitting and looked over at her. "We knit at different tensions. I'm halfway through this and your rows will look different from mine. I'm sorry, but it will be noticeable and it won't look right."

"You're right. My knitting wouldn't look as good as yours."

"Why don't you go upstairs and grab your knitting and I'll help you with that?"

"Maybe tomorrow night, *Mamm.* I'll just sit here and watch you."

Wilma chuckled. "Please yourself. I'm glad for the company."

Chapter 9

On the stroke of three the next afternoon, Florence knocked on the door and Carter stood behind her. She glanced over her shoulder at him. "Are you using me as a shield?"

He smiled and moved forward. "Maybe. Not consciously."

The door opened and Wilma stood there. Judging by her smile she seemed pleased to see them. "Come in. Thank you both for coming."

"How are you, Wilma?" Carter asked, leaning forward to give her a hug.

"Fine."

Then Florence gave her a quick hug before Wilma showed them through to the living room. Levi was on the couch and tried to stand up. Carter said, "No need to get up. It's good to see you, Levi." He reached out his hand and Levi shook it and then Levi nodded a hello to Florence.

"Sit down, both of you," Wilma said.

They sat together on the couch and Wilma sat in a chair next to Levi. "I have made us some hot tea."

"And cookies I see," Carter said.

"*Jah,* the girls made those."

Florence swallowed hard hoping this would go well. All she wanted was to be in charge for the sake of the orchard. Ownership no longer mattered, but her father did want it to continue for generations. She was anxious to hear what Levi had to say.

Suddenly, Wilma stood up and poured everyone a cup of tea. "Help yourself to cream and sugar. Florence, we appreciate the work you've been doing in the orchard these past weeks. I know things have been hard with getting the girls organized."

"You're welcome, and I've been happy to do it. Carter has been wonderful with looking after Iris."

Carter said, "We've both had to juggle a lot of things. Christina has been helping out with her, too."

Levi nodded. "We all have to find a way to get through this together."

"We do," Wilma said.

Once they had their hot tea in one hand and a cookie in the other, Florence began. "I know you said you had some ideas, so do you want to start first, Levi? Or shall I tell you my concerns?"

"You go first, Florence."

"When my father wrote that will, I know he wanted the property and the business to stay in the family for generations. Passed on through my children, or his and Wilma's children. He knew my brothers weren't interested."

"What is your concern, Florence?" Wilma asked. "We're not selling it. You're talking as though we're selling. That idea has been put to bed a long time ago."

"Okay. I won't say more about that topic." Florence shook her head. "I didn't think you were thinking of selling it."

Wilma turned to her husband. "You say your bit now."

"I'm thinking we should have a shared ownership arrangement. Since it belonged to Wilma's first husband and should've gone to you, Florence, I should be left out of any ownership arrangements. And I think you should be the one in total charge of management, Florence, because no one else knows as much as you. That's what I'm told, and I fully believe it."

Florence smiled. That's what she'd wanted. "I can teach whoever is willing to listen."

Levi stroked his graying beard. "I hope the girls are willing to listen. I'd like to learn all I can too."

Florence was both pleased and surprised to hear it. She'd always thought of him as a man who didn't want to be told anything.

"What is this shared ownership arrangement idea, Levi?" Carter asked.

"It's a rough idea that Florence and the other girls share it equally. And I'm not counting Bliss in that. As you said before, Florence, we have to think back to what your *vadder* wanted. He wanted all the girls and Wilma to have a home forever and for the orchard to stay in the family." Then he stared at Florence and she wondered what he was about to say next. "Not to hurt your feelings, but I'm also taking it into consideration he wouldn't have known you'd leave the community."

"That's true," Florence said.

"So, you're saying that Wilma will execute the will, and turn the property over to Florence, and also to her birth-daughters, so they can all own equal shares?" Carter asked.

"That's my idea, with Florence running the place. Or managing the place." Levi looked at his wife. "What do you say?"

"It's fine by me. Will that make you happy, Florence?"

"Yes, if everyone else is happy with it."

"There is one thing, though," Wilma said. "I don't think Cherish should get a share."

Florence kept quiet. Was she saying that because Cherish was the one who found the will? Was she that upset with her?

"And why is that?" Levi asked her.

"Because she already has the farm. Dagmar's farm. She's already told us she's leaving us as soon as she gets the chance."

"It doesn't matter," Levi said. "We can't leave her out. She might get married to someone local and stay on. Who knows what the future holds for her, or any of us? *Nee.* We're not leaving anyone out." Then Levi looked over at Florence. "There is the matter of your brothers. Are you sure they don't want a part of it?"

"I could talk to them again, but they've always said they want nothing to do with it."

"Why don't you talk to them, and then both of you give it some thought?" Levi suggested. "There might be fees for the paperwork for the ownership change if we go down this road."

"I have a friend who's a property lawyer," Carter said. "I'll have a word with him."

"Good."

Wilma stared at Florence. "I know you probably want it all, Florence—everything."

"No, I think it's wonderful what Levi has suggested." Florence smiled at Levi. "Thank you for including me."

"Thank the orchard. She's the one who needs you." Levi chuckled. "Your father knew that."

"Will it all be too much for you?" Wilma asked. "With looking after Iris and your two other orchards?"

Carter answered before Florence had a chance. "She'll manage it all, oversee it, and then we'll have workers do the work. She's not going to do everything herself. That's impossible."

Wilma pressed her lips together. "That's not what I said. I know how many workers an orchard needs and I know things around here have gotten rundown. I was just thinking of Fairfax. He's not bound to work at the dairy any longer. He's been baptized and he's finished his instructions."

"So he's Amish now?" Carter asked.

"That's right and I'm sure he'd love to get back to working for you. He was working for you before, wasn't he?"

"For a little while."

"Briefly," Florence added. "And for his father before that. We'll talk with him soon about it."

Wilma smiled. "Good, but don't tell him I said anything."

"I didn't just hear that," Levi grunted. Then he looked over at Carter and Florence. "Shall we meet again on Wednesday? If we decide we're all in agreement, we'll go ahead."

"Sounds like a good idea," Carter said. "But, could we make it Friday, instead, at this same time?"

"Friday it is," Levi agreed with a firm nod.

Chapter 10

"What do you think about all that?"
Florence asked Carter as soon as they got
in the car.

"That was the best outcome we could hope
for, that's what I think." He pulled her
toward him for a kiss. "Are you happy
with it?"

"I sure am." She snapped her seatbelt on.
"I feel good about it and I'm happy that
Levi wants to learn about the orchard."

Carter started the engine. "A good outcome all around."

"I think so. I'll talk to Mark about it when we collect Iris, and then I'll call Earl tomorrow. I'm positive they won't want a share."

"I'm so happy for you Florence. You finally get what you've always wanted." As they drove out of the orchard, she saw the sign, Baker Apple Orchard, and a tear rolled down her cheek. Even though she'd prayed to get the orchard back, she could never work out how it would happen and to share it with her sisters and have Levi and Wilma's blessing was the best thing ever.

When they turned onto the road, Carter said, "How do you think Wilma felt about it all? I mean, the orchard was hers and now it won't be."

"I don't think she minds. It must be a relief for her that she no longer has to hide the truth. It must've been a burden."

"Maybe."

"Why? What are you thinking?"

"Everything came from Levi. He made all the decisions while she's been the current owner. Ignoring your father's will, of course."

"Yes, but Levi is her husband so she'd have seen it as theirs."

"Okay."

"Her girls are involved and that's enough to make her happy. I think she just didn't want me to own it all. I'm sure my father would be happy with what's been decided."

"Nothing's final yet. Not until a document has been signed."

"I know, but we're halfway there. And it's a miracle we're all in agreement."

"You're right about that. That's a rare thing with so many different personalities involved." Carter laughed. "What about Wilma trying to cut Cherish out?"

"I know. I was shocked, but she was never happy about Dagmar leaving her the farm. She thought it showed favoritism."

"It did."

"I know, but Dagmar wouldn't have cared. She was a very straightforward kind of a woman. Not one to care about people's opinions. She wanted Cherish to have it. She just up and did the legal paperwork, and that was that."

"Good for her. There should be more people like her around. It's not as though Cherish was her child and she chose one over another."

"That's a good way of seeing it. Besides, Dagmar knew Cherish the best out of all of us. They both really got along. It was lovely to see."

"I hope Cherish never learns of her mother's thoughts."

"Me too," agreed Florence. "Let's hope she never finds out."

Chapter 11

While Florence and Carter had been planning for that important meeting with Levi and *Mamm,* Cherish wanted to help Fairfax.

She knew the Millers started milking the cows around four or five in the morning and finished around nine or ten. Then they started over again around four in the afternoon. Between that, they did other jobs, such as fencing, moving the cows between paddocks, and keeping their equipment clean and in good order. Taking all that into account, Cherish figured that she could find him in his sleeping quarters around eleven or twelve, possibly having a rest.

Cherish had Bliss drive her there and she crept onto the Millers' farm. Cherish knew from when Wilma and the girls had visited that Fairfax shared a bedroom with another farm worker. The room was behind the barn.

She hid behind a tree that had a good view of where she was headed. It wasn't long before she saw people heading to the house and Fairfax going into the barn. It was the perfect opportunity.

She knew she wasn't going to get another such opportunity, so she waited until no one was around and she ran to the barn and burst into his room.

When he jumped and turned around to face her, she closed the door behind her.

Cherish stood in front of Fairfax.

"You shouldn't be here," he said.

"Well, I am. I've come to talk with you in private and I can't think where else to do it."

"If people find you in here, they're going to think lots of bad things. You should go."

Cherish lifted her chin in the air. "I'm here about Hope."

His eyebrows flew up. "Is she okay?"

Cherish looked into his eyes. "It depends what you mean by okay."

"Come on," he snapped. "Is she ill?"

"No, but she's unhappy."

"About what? About me?"

"No, not about you exactly, but you have something to do with it."

He swallowed hard. "Just tell me what this is about. Then you can go."

Cherish put her hands on her hips. It was a stance her mother always had when she was cross with her or one of her sisters. "Hey, I'm just trying to help you out."

"Just get on with it, please."

Cherish sat heavily on one of the two beds. "Okay, but this isn't easy to talk about. Firstly, she doesn't know I'm here."

"I kind of guessed that already. I'm guessing no one knows you're here. Is that right?"

"It's not important. She's bothered because you haven't asked her to marry you."

"I have."

"Have you said the words?"

He frowned and was silent for a while. "But she knows we're getting married. We've always talked about it."

Cherish knew exactly what he'd said about marriage going back from the time they'd first met. Hope had told her everything back then. She couldn't allow him to know that, though. "What have you always said? That you'd marry her as soon as you get baptized and have finished the instructions?"

"Exactly. I've always said that." He narrowed his eyes. "She's told you that?"

Cherish ignored his question and threw her hands into the air. "And?"

"And what?"

"You've done both of those and you haven't married Hope."

He frowned again. "If she's expecting me to marry her right now. I can't. How can I? I've no permanent work, no money, and no place to live once I leave the Millers' farm."

"Have you discussed that with Hope?"

"Not that it's any of your business, but Hope's a smart girl. I thought she would've figured that out. She's barely old enough to get married anyway. We'll do it in our timing, Cherish, and not yours." He bounded to his feet and pointed to the door.

Slowly, she rose to her feet and took a step toward the door. "Hey, I'm not the one who made promises I'm not keeping."

"What do you mean?"

Cherish sighed. "Can't you understand what I just said? When you told Hope you'd marry her—"

"Has she changed her mind?"

"Nee! She's worrying that *you* have."

"I'm finding all this a bit difficult." He looked at the floor and rubbed his chin. "Okay," he said looking back at her. "You must have come here for a reason. She must be upset. What do I have to do to fix this?"

"Talk to her. Tell her what you've just told me. That you're waiting to get a job, and a this, and a that, the sky to turn pink. If you're lucky, she'll believe you."

He drew his eyebrows together. "It sounds like you don't believe what I've said?"

"No. I think you're putting things off when it's not necessary."

"I'm not. I told her we'd get married as soon as we can. That means as soon as everything's right and ready to go. She knows this, and if she doesn't know it or think it, she's not being practical and that doesn't sound like Hope. Have you been stirring trouble?"

"*Nee*. How could you even think that?"

He rubbed his chin. "I'm sorry. I shouldn't have said that."

Cherish huffed rather than accept his apology. "When Joy and Isaac got married, they lived with us. When it got too much for them, they got a caravan and put it behind the barn. They lived there all cramped up. But guess what? They were together, and happy, and it didn't matter. What are you waiting for? Life to be perfect? Because life never is perfect. You make do with what you've got and you keep moving forward the best you can."

"That's easy to say when you're young and—"

"Stop!" Cherish stepped closer. If one more person told her she didn't know what she was talking about because she was young, she'd scream. She'd had enough. She turned away from him. "I'm going." She walked to the door saying, "Work things out for yourself." After she put her hand on the door handle, she turned around. "Never tell Hope I was here. She'd die of embarrassment." Then she walked out and closed the door a little too loudly behind herself.

With her hands curled into fists, Cherish walked back to the waiting horse and buggy.

"How did it go?" Bliss asked when she climbed in beside her.

Cherish shook her head at Bliss. "Dreadful. He wouldn't listen."

"Really?"

"Yes. I couldn't get through to him about how Hope felt. I truly think he's going to wait until he has a job and a place to live, and worse, he thinks Hope's too young. I'm sure he hasn't told her that."

"That sounds reasonable, doesn't it?"

Cherish rolled her eyes. "Not to Hope. Now drive!"

"Okay. You don't have to get upset with me." Bliss moved the horse forward.

"I'm not. I'm just upset with Fairfax. I thought he'd listen. I hope I haven't made things worse. What if he thinks Hope sent me there?"

"*Nee.* He wouldn't think that. Hope is not a deceptive person."

Cherish looked at Bliss. Did she mean that she thought she was? "I guess not. Now

I'm wondering why I went to the effort." Cherish threw her hands in the air.

"It wasn't much of an effort."

"It was. I had to sneak into his sleeping quarters. There would've been all kinds of problems if I'd been caught."

"At least you tried. And you did it for a good reason." A car whooshed past them, far too close and startled the horse. "It's okay, boy," Bliss said, talking to him in a calm voice.

"*Denke,* Bliss, for what you said just now."

"He might listen to you."

"I've done all I can. I continually do things for other people and they're not appreciative."

"I appreciate you," Bliss said, as she took a left turn. "You looked after Cottonball so well when I stayed at the hospital with *Dat*."

"I'm not talking about you, but thanks. Nice of you to say so, and all that." Cherish looked out the window at the Millers' cows in the distance.

"I have to get back and help *Mamm* with cleaning. She's complaining about the dust. What do you have to do when we get back?" asked Bliss.

Cherish shook her head. She was in no mood to do anything. "I'm worn out from chores. I think I'll have a slow day."

"Don't you have to help in the orchard?"

"I get a day off today. Let me out at Eddie's place. I have to see what he's doing about Caroline, if anything. She hasn't mentioned him and I'm worried it's all fizzled out."

"Do you want me to come too?"

"*Nee*. Not a chance. One of us should do some chores, don't you think?"

Bliss opened her mouth in shock. "Why does it have to be me?"

"You enjoy it. Besides, I do just as much." Cherish looked over at Bliss's face to see if she'd agree about that. Bliss didn't say anything. "I do," Cherish added.

"Okay."

"I'm glad you agree."

"I don't really. I think we could all do more to help out if I'm truly honest."

"You shouldn't say things like that or people will think you aren't honest most of the time."

"What?"

Cherish sighed. "Never mind. I am helping. I'm helping to get Hope married off and keep her relationship steady and on the right path. Now it's my time to help our lovely neighbor, Eddie. My work is social work. Keeping this family's relationships happy and together. Work is not always work related to chores."

"It's not?"

"Nee."

Bliss screwed up her nose, as she steered the horse to make a right. "But that's not helping the family and it's not getting chores done."

"Exactly. It's way more important." Cherish saw from Bliss's pinched face that she was confused, poor girl. She wasn't the smartest. "You see, if we get Eddie and Caroline together, Caroline will stop making eyes at Adam, and the same with

Fairfax. You should pay attention to how she keeps staring at them whenever they're at the *haus*. If she could, she'd steal one of them away, either from you or Hope. How would you feel if Adam left you for Caroline?"

"Not good, but I can't see that—"

"It's okay for you, but what about Hope? I think if Hope wasn't around, he'd love to see more of Caroline. Is that why Fairfax hasn't made a final commitment to Hope?"

"I don't think so," Bliss said.

"But you don't know for certain. None of us do. But should we risk it?"

Bliss sighed. "Leave things be. Things will work out how they're meant."

"*Nee. Gott* gave me a brain and a mouth and I'm going to use them. There's no harm in Eddie and Caroline forming a friendship, is there?"

Bliss shrugged.

"*Nee*. There's not. As soon as you go home, do lots of chores and don't tell anyone I'm at Eddie's."

"Can I do social chores?"

"Not this time. You'll have to do work ones. We can't both do social chores at the same time otherwise the physical chores would never get done."

Bliss raised her eyebrows. "Where shall I say you are if anyone asks? I don't want to lie. I know for sure they won't think social chores are important."

"Just say you don't know. That won't be a lie because I might've left by the time you get home."

"How will you get home?" Bliss glanced over at her.

"I'll walk."

"Ach jah." Bliss giggled. "It's not far."

"Anyway, no one will ask where I am."

"Mamm might need you to clean." Bliss slowed the horse just as they neared the entrance of the B Right Honey Company.

Cherish held her hands up. "If I'm not there, I'm not there. I'll be here." Sensing Bliss's disapproval, Cherish added, "I'll do double chores tomorrow and the day after."

Bliss nodded and seemed to be satisfied, so when the horse and buggy came to a halt, Cherish jumped out.

Chapter 12

Minutes later, Cherish knocked on the door of Eddie's house.

"I'm coming," a woman called out.

While she waited, she couldn't help noticing that the paint was wearing off the door. It had been painted a pretty turquoise blue and it matched the window frames. Underneath the remaining turquoise paint there was a reddish-brown color, which Cherish guessed was another layer of paint.

Samantha Price

When the door swung open, a smiling middle-aged woman emerged. She wore a simple blue housedress and an apron. From the smell wafting from inside, it seemed she'd been baking. Cherish could tell right away it was Eddie's mother. They had the same dimples in their cheeks and the same oval face.

"Hello, would you be Mrs. ... Eddie's mother?" She suddenly couldn't think of Eddie's last name.

"I am. He's here. Working with the bees. Would you like me to fetch him? I just have to ring the bell and he comes to the house."

"Oh, he's out in the paddocks somewhere?"

"Yes."

Cherish nodded, wondering why she couldn't just call his cellphone. "That's all right. Can I go find him for myself, would that be all right?"

"Sure if you want to. Are you a friend of his?"

"I'm Cherish Baker from the Baker Apple Orchard."

Her face lit up. "Ah, you're one of the Baker girls. I haven't seen you since you were this high. I'd see you with your mother and father at the markets. There were so many of you, all girls. You looked so cute in your tiny bonnets and dresses, and little lace up boots. Simply adorable. I wanted to snatch one of you up and take you home."

Cherish warmed to her right away. "Yes. There are a lot of us. I have five sisters, a half-sister and two half-brothers. Oh, and a stepsister now, too."

"How nice. Eddie's an only child."

Cherish nodded wondering what the appropriate thing was to say.

"Did you know that?" Eddie's mother asked.

"No, I don't think I did."

"Which one are you, then?"

Cherish pointed to herself. "Which one?"

"Yes. In order of birth. Which one?"

"Oh, I'm the youngest."

"The youngest. You'd be so special to your parents."

A giggle escaped Cherish's lips. If only she knew. "Not really. The favorite is Joy. She's the good one. She's married and having a baby soon. I'm the troublesome one."

"Perhaps you're suffering from lack of attention and need to be noticed?"

Cherish was liking this woman more and more. "I think you're right. They say I'm spoiled, but I'm not."

"No. I don't think you are. You have such a kind and sweet face. The face of an angel."

"Thank you." Cherish adjusted her prayer *kapp*. "I should go find Eddie."

"If you don't see him anywhere, come back and you can leave a message for him. Or I could even ring the bell."

Cherish smiled and hoped she wouldn't have a fit of giggles like Bliss had recently. "Okay. Bye, Mrs ... ?"

"Call me Linda."

"Bye, Linda."

Cherish walked away thinking about what Linda had said. It made her feel good that Linda thought she looked like an angel. The chilly breeze bit into Cherish's face as she walked over the slight rise to where the rows of beehives were.

She spotted Eddie in the distance by himself. This was a great opportunity to find out what had been going on and why he and Caroline weren't boyfriend and girlfriend. She really couldn't risk Caroline sticking around the Baker-Bruner place with her roving eyes. As far as Cherish was concerned, Caroline either had to go home or get a boyfriend. She'd had no success trying to get her to go, so Eddie was now her only hope.

He looked up, saw her and gave a wave. He was in his normal clothes; jeans, with a plaid shirt and a straw hat, not in his white beekeeper clothes.

"Hi, Cherish," he called out when they got closer to one another.

"Hello, Eddie."

"What brings you here?"

She walked right up to him. "You do. You bring me here."

He laughed. "What have I done?"

Resting her hands on her hips, she said, "I don't know. You tell me."

He looked down briefly. "There's not much to tell."

"What's going on with you and Caroline?"

"Ah, that. Nothing." He rubbed the back of his neck. "I want to thank you for trying to help a guy like me out, but she wasn't interested at the end of the day."

"What went wrong? I thought everything between the two of you was going well."

"It was until my pa didn't want to go ahead with the tours that she was talking about. We don't need to do it. We're not desperate for money and pa doesn't want people coming here looking around. 'Poking around,' he called it. Thinks they'll sue if they get stung."

"Fair enough, but why should that have anything to do with the way she feels about you?"

He shrugged his shoulders. "You should ask her that."

"No. I know there's more to it." Cherish pointed to a fallen down tree. "Can we sit on that and talk?"

"I wouldn't. Ants have moved into it. I've been meaning to get rid of it. Over here we can sit on the grass and then you can tell me what I've done wrong."

Cherish laughed. He could see straight through her. Eddie sat down first and then Cherish sat cross-legged and pulled her long dress and apron over her knees. They were next to a shed and it gave shelter from the cold wind. "When we were here that time, I could tell she liked you. What happened after that?"

"I can't work it out. Everything was going great for a few days even after I told her about pa not being interested in doing tours."

"Then what came next?" Cherish asked.

He rubbed his chin looking up at the sky. "I asked her out for coffee."

"You what?" Cherish screeched.

His eyes grew wide. "What's wrong with that?"

"Coffee?"

"Yes. I didn't see any harm in it. Is there?"

"It's so wrong on so many levels. I thought you knew how this was going to work. I told you *not* to let her know you're interested. Then you turn around and ask her to have coffee with you." Cherish grunted.

"It was only coffee. I didn't think that would matter." He grimaced. "I understand what you're saying to a point, but there comes a time where she's got to know I'm interested. How could we have a relationship otherwise?"

Cherish groaned. "You didn't listen to anything I said. I told you not to let her know you like her. Now she knows you do, and she'd be offended you didn't invite her to dinner. It's all wrong. All my hard work ruined just like that." Cherish snapped her fingers in the air. No wonder he didn't have a girlfriend.

"Um. What hard work did you do?" Eddie asked. "I haven't seen you for weeks."

"Preparation work." She plucked a blade of grass. "I don't know how you're going to come back from this."

"I'd be grateful if you could think of something. She did seem interested, before she wasn't. I mean before she knew I was."

"See? I told you so." Cherish stroked the blade of grass across her chin. "Now I have to come up with another plan."

"What if she sees me with another girl?" he suggested.

Cherish leaned over and slapped his shoulder. "Brilliant. That's perfect."

He made a face and rubbed his shoulder. "Ow. You're stronger than you look."

"Thanks. It's all the chores they make me do. Scrubbing floors and all that. Down on my hands and knees. It's so hard."

"That's awful."

"I know but someone has to do it. I'm the youngest so it falls to me. It's okay. I'm used to it. Anyway, do you know anyone who could be your fake girlfriend?"

He shook his head. "I told you before, I never meet anyone."

"What about when you're called out for hive removals?"

He shook his head again. "All old people for some reason."

Cherish pulled another blade of grass while she thought. "You don't have to have a real girlfriend, as long as Caroline thinks you have one. When she hears about the new and very attractive woman in your life, she'll be upset that you aren't crying into your soup about her rejecting you."

He wrinkled his nose. "How will this work?"

"I'll casually mention that I saw you with a girl, a young woman. I have a shift Thursday at the coffee shop. When I get home, I'll say you were there with a very attractive blonde woman and she was all over you."

His face lit up. "I like the sound of that."

"Hopefully, Caroline won't like the sound of it and you might get a visit from her the day after. I'd be looking good if I were you." She looked down at what he was wearing. "Scrub yourself up and put on your best working clothes. Shave."

He rubbed his stubbly chin. "Some girls like this nearly-there beard look."

She grimaced. "No. They don't."

"Oh. I thought they did."

"Not Caroline."

"Okay. I'll do whatever you say."

"Good. I wish there were more people like you around."

He laughed. "You're funny, Cherish."

"Just listen up. Don't mind me. Get your mind on Caroline. When she comes here, be friendly, but not over friendly. Maybe ask what she's doing and don't be too interested in the answer. If she says she's changed her mind about coffee, you tell her things have changed. You've met someone else."

He frowned. "How's that going to work? This is where I get confused."

"Trust me. You won't be able to get rid of her. Girls like her can't take rejection. She has to win you, and you have to play hard to get."

"I dunno, Cherish. I want her to like me for me."

"She will. And she'll like you even more for you if she thinks other girls do too. Get it?"

"Not really, but I know nothing about this kind of thing. I'll do what you say and I'll hope it works. It worked to start with between me and her, before things fizzled."

"Don't weaken when she says she's changed her mind about coffee. You have to say no."

"It's going to be hard. I'm not sure if I can say no to her."

Cherish jabbed her finger in the air at him. "You can and you will. You'll have to or it'll be all over." When he seemed unsure, she added, "The path of love is not often a smooth one."

He smiled. "I'm finding that out. How do you know so much?"

"I watch and I observe."

A bell sounded and Eddie jumped to his feet.

"What's that?" Cherish asked.

"It's Ma. It's either someone on the phone for me or she's made me a cup of coffee."

Cherish stood. "Don't you have a cellphone?"

"Yeah, but Ma doesn't like them. She prefers the old ways."

"The old ways, meaning ringing a bell?"

He chuckled. "It works."

"It would get annoying after a while. Ding a ling, a ling. A ling. Ring, ring. Ding, ding, ding."

"It is annoying when you do it." He laughed. "It doesn't bother me at all. Will you stay and have some coffee? You can meet Ma."

"I met your mother. She's really nice. I would stay longer, but I've got chores. Don't forget, Thursday night I'll be telling Caroline I saw you with a girl. I reckon she'll come and see you the very next day, Friday. Be prepared and think before you speak. Also don't stare at her."

"I will, Cherish, thanks." They started walking toward the house and the bell sounded again. "What happens when Caroline finds out the truth, that there is no other woman?"

"She won't. Anyway, it's not a lie. I'll see you with a waitress, being waited on. All the waitresses at my work have blonde hair. Oh wait, you won't really be there, will you?"

Eddie laughed. "I could be. I'll be in town on Thursday getting supplies. I could swing by, so you won't be telling her a total lie."

She was pleased to see he had morals—partial ones, anyway. "Okay. Great idea. If that's what you want."

"Why not? It can't hurt."

"I'll see you Thursday. My shift is between ten and four."

"I'll be there. Hey, would you like me to drive you home from the café on Thursday? I could get there at three thirty."

"I'd love that. Thanks. I'll see you soon."

"Great." They parted ways. He headed to his house and she walked back to the road. "Thanks again, Cherish," he called out.

She looked back and waved.

Chapter 13

The next day, Cherish was helping Levi and the girls tidy the barn to get ready for Florence to take over. The barn, like so many other things around the orchard, had been neglected. It was dirty, dusty, and disorganized.

When Cherish heard hoofbeats, she looked out and saw Ada's horse and buggy coming toward the house. "It's Ada," Cherish told everyone.

"She might've heard the news," Levi said, from his chair where he was directing the girls and telling them what to do.

"Do you mean the news about what was decided about the orchard?" Cherish asked.

"*Jah.*"

Had Ada recovered from being uninvited? She hadn't been to the house since her and Bliss's visit. More than anything, Cherish wanted to find out what was going on. "I'll help her with the horse," said Cherish, hurrying out of the barn.

She walked over just as Ada was getting out. "Hi, Ada. Shall I put the horse in the paddock for you?"

"*Nee.* I won't be staying long."

That wasn't a good sign. She normally stayed for most of the day whenever she visited. As she looped the reins over the post, she looked over Cherish's shoulder. "A cleaning bee, is it?"

"That's right. We're getting organized for winter."

"It's already winter."

"That's right.

Ada squinted as she stared into the barn through the open door. "Levi's in there too?"

"*Jah*. Do you want me to fetch him for you?"

"*Nee*. I think I should talk to your *mudder* alone."

Ada made to walk away, but Cherish asked, "Is everything okay?"

Ada stopped still and then turned to face her. "Everything is fine. Why do you ask?"

Cherish shrugged. "I'm not sure."

Ada flung a hand toward the barn. "Go help your family. Get your chores done. I know you're trying to get out of work by prolonging a conversation with me."

Cherish's eyes opened wide. "I'm not."

"Good. Then go." Ada then folded her arms and leaned back, looking down her nose at Cherish.

Cherish had no choice but to walk back to the barn. She set about moving some things around, but then she couldn't help herself any longer. "How about I bring everyone cups of hot chocolate?" she called out over the noise of the buzz of conversation.

Levi said, "You might as well. You're not really doing anything here. Don't take any longer than need be."

"I'll help you," said Bliss, who'd been trying to move a hay bale by herself.

"*Nee,*" Levi said. "It's not a job that takes two."

Cherish hurried out of the barn, then she slipped into the mud room at the back of the house. It shared a wall with the kitchen. She moved to the wall and pressed her ear against it.

The first voice she heard was Ada's. "Don't you think you should've asked me first?"

"Nothing's been decided yet, not completely."

"I can see it's a tough and complicated situation. One that would require a lot of prayer."

"We have prayed about it," Wilma told her. "I'm sorry that you were invited and then told you couldn't come."

"I was hurt. You've always asked me about things in the past, and that's why it took me by surprise and you sent Cherish, of all people."

Cherish's mouth dropped open. What did Ada mean by that?

"Bliss was with her. I sent the two of them."

"Something doesn't sound right. I'm guessing Levi didn't want Samuel and I here, is that right?"

There was some hesitation before *Mamm* spoke. "It's a thing that just needed to be talked about between the four of us."

"And, do you think you were capable of making or contributing to a decision. You know you haven't made the best choices in the past."

"I know, that's true, but I'd like to fix that. I believe that Levi is a good man and he will guide me to make a decision that will benefit everyone."

"From the way you're talking, I have to guess that no decision was made at all yesterday."

"Um, we did talk some things through. Carter is checking on fees and things for changing ownership over."

"Ownership to whom?" Ada asked.

Cherish knew from the way her mother was speaking so carefully, that she didn't want to discuss it just yet. Or perhaps Levi had asked her not to talk about anything until a decision had been made. She was just about to burst through the door to help her mother out by interrupting them, when her mother spoke.

"The main thing is, I'm left out of everything."

"Oh, that hardly seems fair. What about Levi?" Ada asked.

"Him too."

Ada huffed. "Then who ...?"

"Florence and my girls. Florence even wanted Bliss to have a share. Can you believe it?"

"That is odd. She's not even a Baker, she's a Bruner."

"I know," *Mamm* said angrily. "I told them not to worry about Cherish, because she's got the farm, but they all insisted she be included."

Cherish covered her mouth. Her mother wanted to leave her out entirely? How was that fair? It was hurtful.

Ada went on to tell *Mamm* she should've been there to talk some common sense. She was siding with her mother against her. Why did everyone hate her?

Tears streamed down Cherish's face and she ran out of the mud room allowing the door to bang behind her. She ran out into the orchard until she was out of breath. Then she slumped to the cold ground.

Why was her mother so mean?

If her mother didn't even love her, how would anyone?

A minute later, Cherish heard panting in her ear. She looked up to see Caramel. She sat up and hugged him to herself. "You're the only one who cares about me. We should run away. Go to the farm, now."

Caramel looked over his shoulder. Then Cherish heard a twig breaking. It was Levi walking through the orchard. She let go of Caramel and dried her eyes as she stood up. "Are you supposed to be walking?"

"I saw you running away from the *haus* and the dog and I decided we'd best check on you. What's happened?"

She blew out a deep breath. "I heard *Mamm* saying she didn't want me to have anything to do with the orchard. I don't really want a share, but she should've wanted me to have one. She's my mother."

Slowly Levi nodded. "I know how you feel, but she has a different opinion. *Gott* has already blessed you."

"You don't agree with her, though?"

He shook his head. *"Gott* can bless you twice."

That made Cherish smile and it made her like Levi a tiny bit more, even though she didn't want to.

"Denke, Levi." She sniffed, and then Caramel licked her hand.

"Let's go back to the barn. Working will keep your mind off things."

"Okay."

As they walked back, Levi gently put a hand on her shoulder. "Sometimes people disappoint us. And at other times we'll be the ones doing the disappointing. Don't hold a grudge in your heart."

His words made sense. She knew she was a disappointment to her mother because of the things she'd done. "I'll try my best not to. But, it's not going to be easy."

Chapter 14

Late that night when the girls were outside and Wilma was alone knitting in the living room, Cherish approached her mother to have an honest talk. After she sat on the opposite couch, she asked, "Has Levi gone to bed already?"

Her mother stopped knitting and looked up. "You know he has. He said goodnight and you took his teacup from him only a half hour ago."

"Oh, that's right."

Wilma resumed her knitting.

Cherish didn't want to talk about the thing that hurt her, but she wanted to know why her mother was so mean. She took a deep breath and then spoke. *"Mamm,* I know you don't want me to have any part of the orchard."

Wilma stopped knitting once more, looked up at her and blinked rapidly. "Who told you that?"

"I overheard you telling Ada. I just want to know why." It didn't miss Cherish's notice that Levi hadn't told Wilma that she knew this. Didn't a husband and wife tell each other everything?

"Don't look at me as though I'm awful," Wilma said. "It was for practical reasons only. You have your aunt's farm. She left it to you and you alone. What need would you have of an orchard?"

"It's a part of an orchard and I'm just as entitled to my share same as Mercy and Honor. They've not been here since you married Levi. They might never come back here. Why not cut them out?" Cherish put her feet up on the coffee table.

Wilma growled, "Get off that."

Cherish removed her feet and then sat up straight.

Wilma tilted her head back as she continued to stare at Cherish. "I want Mercy and Honor to have something. Why shouldn't they?"

"They have their own families and their own husbands. Their husbands work." Cherish tugged on the strings of her *kapp* in frustration. "Look. I'm not saying cut Mercy and Honor out, I'm just wondering why you said to cut me out."

"I just told you. That's my opinion and I'm entitled to have one. You and I often don't agree on things and this is no different. I do think it's unfair of Dagmar to have left you that farm when you have siblings. It was awful. So unthinking and so unkind of her. But since she spent her adult life unmarried she was used to not thinking of others."

"She knew me. She didn't really know anyone else. Not really. That's why. That's what she wanted." She bit her lip to keep from telling *Mamm* that she didn't seem to care what anyone else wanted, either. *Mamm* didn't care what *Dat* had wanted so it was only to be expected that *Mamm* wouldn't care what Aunt Dagmar wanted.

"I've got nothing left to say. You asked me and I told you. I'm not going to apologize for something that makes perfect sense to me."

"I'm glad to know that's how you feel. I will be leaving for the farm as soon as I'm able. It's clear I'm not cared for around here." Cherish ran out of the room, up the stairs and closed herself in her bedroom. She flopped down on her bed. How could her mother be so different from her? Looking up at the ceiling she thought about all the things she'd miss when she left. She'd miss her room, the view from her room that spread along the barn and down to the road, her sisters, the constant flow of visitors, but she wouldn't miss being told what to do.

There was a knock on her bedroom door and then it started opening. She jumped off her bed hoping it wasn't Wilma.

She'd said all she had to say to her.

When Bliss appeared, Cherish was relieved and pulled the door open wider.

"What's wrong?" Bliss whispered.

Cherish closed the door and then sat down on her bed. "It's just *Mamm*. She wants me left out of the orchard arrangement. I don't really care, and that's the truth, but it's just the thought of being deliberately left out. And, by my own mother."

Bliss sat next to her. "I know. I heard. Florence and Carter thought I should have a share. That was nice of them. It was nice to think that someone wanted me included."

Cherish put her arm around her. "It's awful to feel left out, isn't it?"

Bliss nodded. "I don't feel I should have a share and neither does *Dat*. It's not mine, never has been. It belongs to the Bakers."

"Why is life so complicated, Bliss?"

"Because everyone has a different opinion."

"*Jah,* you're right. I didn't expect you to answer that. It seems it's true, especially everyone who lives in this *haus.* I just can't wait to leave. Should I run away now?"

"*Nee.* They'd only find you and bring you back. *Dat* is not supposed to worry or get stressed, remember?"

"*Jah,* I'm sorry! I forgot." Cherish flung herself back all the way until she was lying across her bed.

Bliss did the same. "Just wait patiently until you're old enough. It's not that long to wait. If you leave now you might regret it. Besides, I'd miss you."

Cherish couldn't help smiling. At least someone wanted her around.

Chapter 15

The next day, Hope was halfway through the midday meal when *Mamm* looked out the kitchen window and announced that Fairfax was outside.

Hope walked to the door, straightening her *kapp* and smoothing down her apron. When she opened the door, her excitement over his unexpected visit changed to worry.

He looked like he hadn't slept in a week. His black hat was held against his chest and his hair was messy, and his normally tanned complexion was pallid.

"Is something wrong?" she asked.

"No. Can we sit out here and talk?" He cocked his head to one side motioning toward the two porch chairs.

Hope was relieved no one had died and nothing was wrong, but there had to be something going on. She looked over to the side at the chairs he'd been looking at when he spoke. He was definitely avoiding looking her in the eyes. "We're just having a meal. There's plenty if you'd like to join us."

"No. I've eaten. *Denke.*" He brushed his fair hair to one side and placed his hat on his head.

She walked over to the chairs and sat down on one of them.

When he sat next to her, he bumped his knee on hers. "Is everything all right with us?"

Now he was looking in her eyes, but she wasn't liking what he said. "Of course." Why would he ask such a thing? "Isn't it?"

"You tell me."

"I think it is. Why do you ask? You're scaring me."

"Why aren't you working at Jane's today?"

"It's a slow time of year and Jane said not to come in. She's using this time to get more rooms repainted. Why do you ask?"

"Just wondering."

"Tell me why you're asking all these things."

"Hope, I told you we'd get married and I don't appreciate being pressured. I've joined the community for you, I've suffered the stench of the cows and getting kicked by one or two of them every day. I've survived the early mornings, I've changed my whole way of life for you. This is a whole new world for me and I'm sorry if I'm not moving fast enough for you."

Hope froze, not game to say a word because he seemed so upset. Somehow she knew Cherish was behind this. If only she had kept her feelings to herself, but it was hard when she was so upset.

Lines appeared in his forehead. "I need some space to breathe. I was warned this would happen." He straightened his back and looked past her.

"Who warned you about what?"

He shook his head. "I was told not to join the community for love. The bishop said it early on. Months ago. Love is one thing, but this is the rest of my life we're talking about."

"I still don't know what you're saying. What did you say to the bishop for him to tell you that?"

"That's not the point. You're pressuring me to marry you right away. I'm not ready, we're not ready. You're barely seventeen."

"Almost eighteen."

"Not for a while."

"All my older sisters got married young."

"You don't have to do what they did. Why the rush? I said we'd marry. I'm here, aren't I?"

She couldn't speak. Didn't he want to be married to her as soon as he could? "A few months ago, you said you wanted to marry as soon as possible—as soon as we're able. What's changed?"

He counted them all on his fingers as he spoke. "No job, no place to live, no transportation, you're not eighteen." He put his hand down. "Shall I go on?"

She tugged at her high neckline, feeling she was choking. "So you meant, as soon as possible, as long as all those conditions are met?"

"Yes. As soon as I leave the Millers,' I'll have no place to lay my head, and I won't have use of one of their buggies."

It hurt Hope to hear him talk like this, but she had to find out the answer to her next question. "Well, what are you doing about it?"

He bounded to his feet. "I'm doing a lot about it, but I don't need pressure from you while I sort things out."

She stood up too. "I'm not pressuring you. I just need to know when we'd move forward with things. I've said nothing."

"Yes, you said nothing to me, but you send your little mouthpiece instead."

Her eyebrows drew together and then she realized she was correct about what had happened. "Cherish."

He pointed at her. "See? You admit it. We need to have some space for a few days, Hope."

"Are we, do you still ..."

"Everything's okay. We'll be okay, but I just need a few days by myself to think things through." He turned on his heel and walked away.

She watched in shock as he strode away and then climbed into his borrowed buggy. He didn't even look back at her when he moved the horse and buggy down the driveway away from the house.

Hope sat down in the porch chair holding her head as the clip-clopping of the horse's hooves faded into nothingness.

What had just happened? Were her memories distorted? He'd always said they'd marry as soon as they were able.

The front door opened and out of the corner of her eye, she saw someone rushing toward her.

"Why did Fairfax leave so quickly?"

Hope heard Cherish's voice, but she was still staring at nothing, in shock.

Cherish grabbed her arm. "Hope!"

"Jah?" Hope felt lightheaded, as though she might faint.

"What happened?"

Hope slowly turned to look at her youngest sister, the troublemaker, the loose-lipped one of the family. "I told you not to say anything. I don't know what you said to him, but he is convinced I sent you there. There was no point telling him I had nothing to do with it." She buried her face in her hands. "He was too angry."

Cherish clapped her hand over her mouth. "Oh no. I told him not to say anything. I was only trying to help. I'm so sorry."

Hope nodded. "Don't worry. I'm not upset with you. I know you were trying to be helpful. I'm disappointed with him. He should've known I wouldn't scheme behind his back and send you there."

Cherish sat down next to her. "What did he say?"

"He said I was pressuring him to marry, or some such thing, and that he needed a few days away from me so he could think."

Cherish bit her lip, feeling like the worst sister in the world. "I feel so bad. I never should've gone there."

"Too late for that."

"It's good how you're not crying about this. I'd be really upset."

"If he needs a few days to think about our relationship, so do I. Why would I want to marry someone who's not sure he wants to marry me?"

"He does, though. He's in love with you. You two are perfect together. He might be just tired or something. Having a bad day, maybe."

"I don't know." Hope straightened her apron over her knees. "I have a lot to consider."

Cherish was worried about how calm Hope was. Any other of her sisters, except for

Joy, would be throwing herself around in despair. Hope was strangely calm.

"Don't tell anyone about this, will you?"

"Like who?" Cherish asked.

"I don't want Caroline to find out or she'd think she has a chance with him."

"I won't say anything."

"But can you keep your mouth shut this time?" Hope glared at Cherish.

"Of course. I don't want Caroline to even think about Fairfax. I've got a plan for her and Eddie the beekeeper."

"That's right. I forgot about that completely. How's that coming along?"

Cherish was pleased Hope wasn't looking so angry with her now. "We might know more tonight. I think she forgot about him, but I'm hoping that will all change soon— over dinner."

"Just be careful. I don't want anything to backfire on you."

"It won't. Don't worry. And don't worry about Fairfax. He's probably just feeling the pressure of how everything in his life is new. His mom and dad have moved away, he adjusted to being with the Millers and now he has to leave them and find some other work and some other place to live. And a horse and buggy—all that costs money and how much does he have?"

"None. But he's got me. I would've thought that would've made up for everything. We can marry and move here just like how Joy and Isaac started their married life."

"Men are strange. I know he loves you. He always has. Don't let go of that, Hope."

Hope slowly nodded and looked away. "If you don't mind, I'd like to be alone right now. I'll sit here in the fresh air for a moment. Keep everyone away from me. Don't tell anyone what happened."

"Sure." Cherish stood up and then gave Hope a hug before she hurried into the house.

Chapter 16

On Thursday, Eddie arrived at the café just when Cherish was about to finish her shift. He waved and walked over to her while she wiped down one of the tables. By this time of the afternoon the lunch trade had moved on. There was one man drinking coffee and engrossed in his laptop computer, and another on the other side of the room talking loudly on his cellphone. Cherish often wished Rocky would make a rule that there were no cellphones allowed in the café. People were on them constantly even when they were with other people at a table.

"I meant to get here earlier," Eddie blurted out as he pulled off his knitted cap.

"No hello, how are you?"

He smiled. "Sorry. Hello, and how are you?"

"I'm fine, and you?"

He straightened up. "Anxious."

"About what?"

"About Caroline of course. Remember, I'm supposed to be here at the café with another woman."

Cherish laughed. "You are. It's me. I'm another woman."

"Yeah, well just don't tell her that."

"I won't. And she mustn't see that you've driven me home either. I'll have to get out up the road and walk back."

"Okay. I just hope it doesn't rain. There's rain clouds everywhere."

Cherish turned around and looked at the clock that was positioned just above the coffee machine. Three o'clock exactly. Finishing time for her. She turned back to Eddie. "You don't want anything, do you?"

"I've been looking forward to the lemon cake."

"My treat. I'll get a piece for you to go."

He looked down at the chairs and table in between them. "Okay."

Cherish could see he wanted to sit down, but she didn't have time for small talk. She couldn't wait to get home and tell Caroline that she'd seen Eddie. "Where's your car?"

"Parked right outside."

"Wait in it and I'll be out in a minute."

"Okay." He pulled his cap back on and headed outside.

Cherish busied herself with arranging a slice of lemon cake into a takeout container. She also asked Jen, the barista, for a black take-out coffee. She'd completely forgotten to ask him if he wanted something to drink. While the barista was making the coffee, Cherish put the money in the till. Then she put on her coat and grabbed her bag.

When the coffee was ready, she took a hold of it along with the cake and said goodbye to her co-workers. The man on the cellphone had hurried to open the café door for her. Cherish was surprised he even noticed what was going on around him.

She thanked him and he gave her a beaming smile.

Eddie was leaning on his car smoking, and when he saw Cherish he threw the cigarette onto the footpath, stubbed it out with his shoe and then opened the passenger-side door for her.

"Thank you." Before he reached the driver's side, she'd placed the coffee in the cupholder and placed the cake on the back seat. "I got you a coffee," she said once he was seated.

"I'm fine, thanks."

"What? You don't want it?"

"Not really. Do you want it?"

Cherish shrugged her shoulders. "Okay." Just as well she'd gotten the kind of coffee she wanted.

"Thanks anyway," he said.

Cherish looked at the car's dashboard where the cupholder popped out when a button was pressed. "What a great idea this cupholder is. I need one in our buggy. When I'm old enough to have my own buggy, I'm going to make sure it has one. As well as a heater."

"Are you too cold, because I can turn the air conditioner warmer."

"I'll live. This is a nice car for a beekeeper."

When Eddie laughed, she realized what a stupid thing she'd said.

"I'm sorry, I just meant that ... I thought you had a pickup truck."

"Pa owns that. I drive it sometimes. I like a nice car."

"Good."

Once they were about a mile along the road, Eddie said, "What are you going to say to Caroline exactly?"

"Just what I said. I've seen you with someone." She drew her hands to her heart. "Oh, she'll be so jealous that you forgot about her so suddenly and now you have someone else. And your 'someone else' is real pretty, too."

"Yeah?" He chuckled.

"She sure is."

"How pretty?"

"Nearly perfect. And she has a lovely nose."

He laughed again "Yeah, because that's so important in an imaginary girlfriend. You'll have to call me as soon as you can to let me know what happens. You still have my cell number?"

"I sure do. I'll call you. I have a good feeling about this."

"Me too."

Once Cherish got home, she pieced together a plan for the dinner conversation that would take place that night. She enlisted Hope's help again, since Hope would benefit once Eddie and Caroline became a couple.

Chapter 17

Over dinner, Levi announced to everyone that Carter and Florence were coming at three the next day to finalize things, finally, about the orchard. He asked everyone to give them some privacy, and find something to do away from the house.

Hope said just what she'd been told to say. "Cherish, how was your work today? You were at the café, weren't you?"

"I had a really good day. I saw Eddie, the beekeeper."

Caroline looked up. "Where did you see him?"

Cherish knew her plan was working already. "He came into the café today. He's hooked on the lemon cakes. They are delicious— everyone thinks so."

"What was he doing there, apart from eating cake?" Hope asked, just as Cherish had instructed her.

Cherish shrugged her shoulders. "He was with some girl. They looked pretty cozy too."

"Oh. I didn't know Eddie had a girlfriend," said Hope.

"No, he doesn't," Caroline snapped. "He asked me out only recently and I said no."

"It seems someone else has snapped him up." Cherish could barely keep the smile from her face. "She's really pretty too. They looked really good together. He's tall with dark hair, she was tall too, but with blonde hair. They were perfect together. And, he's so nice and he looked so happy. I couldn't stop looking at them they looked so good together."

"You've said she's pretty twice," Caroline told her.

"It must be true, then." Cherish had another mouthful of pea and ham soup. When she looked up at Caroline, she was glad to see her looking confused. She really couldn't say anything else without appearing too obvious.

Wilma butted in, talking about something altogether different and saving Cherish from having to change the subject herself. "When Florence was here, she said we need to start using that fruit we have stored. We need to make an effort to do what we used to do. We used to cook all day, remember? When you girls weren't helping in the orchard or at the stall or the shop, we'd be cooking. Florence was very upset to see our stocks in the supply room so low."

"We could do that," said Hope. "I'll help as much as I can while Jane's getting her rooms painted. It's a slow time of year."

"You were supposed to leave that job, Hope. Cherish, you were supposed to leave your job at the café." Levi glared at the two of them. "We need your help here at the orchard."

It was the same old complaint Cherish had heard dozens of times before. "I'm only doing one shift a week. That's practically nothing. Only a few hours. I'm using that in place of my free time."

"You need to be driven in and driven back home. That takes one of us away from the orchard," Levi said.

"She has cut down," Wilma told him.

"So have I," Hope added. "Jane is still looking for someone to replace me but she hasn't been able to find anyone."

Wilma narrowed her eyes. "I find that hard to believe, Hope. You're just a cleaner. There would be dozens of women looking for a job like that."

Hope shrugged her shoulders. "I would've thought so too. I'm just going by what Jane has told me."

"We can work later into the night after the evening meal," Cherish suggested.

"*Jah*, but will you?" Levi stared at Cherish.

"We will. I will."

"Me too," added Hope.

"I'll do it in the daytime," Bliss said. "No use too many of us being in the kitchen at the same time."

Wilma clapped her hands together. "Hope and Cherish, you can work in the orchard during the day doing whatever Florence tells you and at night you can cook. I'll have a list of things ready for you to make."

"I can cope with that." Cherish smiled.

"Sounds good to me too." Hope helped herself to a second helping of soup.

Levi set his spoon down and interlaced his fingers, and set his hands on the table. "Caroline, Favor, and Bliss, you can work in the shop and in the orchard too. When it's not busy, it really only needs one of you in the shop. When you're not in the shop, you'll be doing chores. The days of you girls lazing about the house or off with your friends are over."

"Yes, and if the shop gets busy when there's only one person there, we can have a bell and ring it." Cherish couldn't help smiling at the first suggestion she'd ever had.

Levi smiled. *"Wunderbaar.* I like that idea. I think I have a brass bell somewhere in the barn."

"Why would you have a bell?" *Mamm* stared at Levi.

"I'm not sure. It belonged to some relative or other. Great thinking, Cherish. I feel we're all getting more organized and that's what this place needs. Soon, we're having another meeting with Carter and Florence and even more plans will be put into place. We're organizing a new ownership arrangement."

"What will it be, *Dat?*" Bliss asked.

"I can't say until I meet with them."

Cherish said, "So ... does that mean we'll be doing more work, or less?"

Wilma glared at her. "It won't make any difference to what we have planned for you. Expect that you'll be working harder than ever. Especially since you refuse to give up the café work. Bliss has left off, so it can't be hard for you to do the same."

Cherish hung her head. She really had nothing to say. All she knew was that the few hours she spent a week at the café was the only thing keeping her sane. That's how it felt. She loved being with her co-workers, sharing a laugh and getting to know them better. Then there were the regulars at the café. They all loved her. Everyone did, including the new boss, Rocky. At work, she wasn't treated like an annoying child. She was respected as a person and that made her feel good. Cherish looked at all the people around the table. They all should treat her better.

When Caroline and Favor were given the job of cleaning up after dinner, the other girls went out to sit on the porch in the chilly night air.

Bliss, Cherish and Hope sat on the top step, with Cherish in the middle.

"I can't work out why Caroline's still here," Cherish grumbled.

"They actually believe her house burned down," said Hope.

"But still ... are we taking in charity cases now?" Cherish asked.

Bliss gasped. "Oh, that's a rude thing to say. People can't help it if they need charity. One day it could be you, Cherish."

"Yeah, well, I must be a rude person. I can't help it if I'm annoyed. They're giving her chores as though she's one of us, but she's not. She's not even in the community, yet she goes to all the meetings and the singings and no one says one thing. Oh, poor little girl your fake house has fake burned down. Boo Hoo!"

Hope said, "She's here, so we just have to cope the best we can."

"I like her," Bliss mumbled.

Cherish bumped Bliss's shoulder. "You like everyone."

Bliss bumped her back. "That's a good thing, not a bad thing. Everyone is good in their own way."

Cherish shrugged. "I've only got a couple more years until I escape to the farm. I'd like to enjoy those last two years with my family. Hope, you'll be leaving to get married soon, and right now I'm missing out on time with Favor. I feel Caroline will be here forever. *Mamm* and Levi don't seem to be in a hurry for her to leave." Cherish blew out a deep breath. "I mean, is she paying board? No. Even though her parents are rich."

"She's doing lots of work here though," Bliss pointed out.

"Yeah, but it's not enough to make up for all the food she's eating. Did you see how much she scarfed down at dinner just now? And she stuck her fork in the last buttered potato just as I was reaching for it with my fork. I nearly stabbed her hand. Lucky I stopped myself. I really wanted that potato."

A giggle escaped Bliss's lips. "I didn't know you like potatoes that much."

"I do. I love them. I could eat them all day and nothing else."

"I wasn't looking at how much or how many potatoes she was eating. And, Cherish, I don't think I'll be leaving to get married. I fear it's all over between me and Fairfax. He came to this community for nothing. All he's done is get my hopes up and caused me to build dreams in my head. I'm preparing myself for the crash when he dumps me."

Bliss leaned across Cherish. "What do you mean?"

Cherish told her, "He said he needs time apart. A few days to clear his head. They had a tiny disagreement. It wasn't much at all."

"You weren't supposed to say anything, Cherish," Hope told her.

"Not to Caroline, but you don't mind me saying something to Bliss, surely?"

"It's okay, but not a word to Caroline," Hope whispered. "Or anyone else, Cherish."

"I won't say a thing."

"Me either," said Bliss.

Cherish continued, telling Bliss, "It was my fault all this happened. Hope was worried about where things were going. I talked to Fairfax to make him see what he was doing, and I made things worse."

"Yeah," Hope said, "talked to him without me knowing and he thinks I sent her."

Bliss covered her mouth while her eyes opened wide. "This is dreadful."

Hope sighed. "There's nothing anyone can do now. We just have to wait and see how things develop."

Bliss leaned across Cherish and rubbed Hope's shoulder. "I'm so sorry, Hope. It'll come right, though. He loves you. I can tell."

Cherish sighed and leaned back so Bliss had to move her arm. "Life and love can be so difficult. Look at the path the orchard has taken. It was *Dat's* and then it was *Mamm's* but it wasn't supposed to be hers. It was meant to be Florence's then ... who knows where it will end up?"

Hope hugged her knees to herself. "It seems nothing in life is certain."

"Nothing unless *Gott* wills it," Bliss added.

"I wonder what *Gott* wants for each of us. How would we know we're making the right decisions with things?"

The front door swung open and Favor and Caroline stepped out.

Cherish stood up when the two girls walked toward them, allowing Favor and Caroline space to walk down the stairs. "That clean-up was fast."

"We're fast workers."

"I hope so. Or, maybe it wasn't done properly, hmmm?" Cherish knew that was enough to start an argument, but something had forced her to say it.

"We did everything," Favor told her.

Caroline walked down the steps ignoring everyone, and then walked around the corner while lighting a cigarette.

She never usually smoked when Levi and Wilma were still awake. Favor hurried around the corner to be with Caroline.

Cherish sat back down. "See? Favor never talks to me anymore. Not more than three or four words at a time. It's like I don't exist anymore."

Hope patted Cherish's arm. "Don't worry. She won't be here forever. Just think of it this way, if she wasn't here you'd be doing more chores."

"I guess you're right about that. I suppose there is an upside, a very small one."

"Don't let her bother you, Cherish. She's really okay when you talk with her. She's a good person deep down."

"Let's just hope that Adam doesn't agree with you, Bliss." Cherish stared at Bliss wondering how she'd react to that.

Bliss just smiled. "I'm not worried. If Adam likes her better than me, he's not the right man for me. I'd be happy for them if they were happy. She'd join the community and that would have to be a blessing for everyone."

Cherish stared at her stepsister, wondering how she could be so nice. Then she turned to Hope, who was still sitting on her opposite side. "What do you think about that, Hope?"

"Bliss is right. It's a good way to view things. I can only be who I am, and if that's not good enough for Fairfax there's nothing I can do about it."

"That's right. It's a matter of letting him find his feet in his new life," Bliss said.

"It's just that things are different from how I imagined them. I thought we'd be married as soon as possible and ... I hadn't even given any thought to where we'd live, but I'm sure he won't find it hard getting work anywhere."

Bliss said, "He does have experience in quite a few areas. That's got to count for something."

Cherish looked at the smoke floating around the corner of the house. It was lighted up by the gaslighting glowing from the kitchen window. The smell was so strong she was certain Levi and Wilma would smell it every evening, yet they weren't doing a thing about it.

Caroline could probably murder someone and get away with it.

Chapter 18

On Friday, Florence and Carter were back at the Baker Apple Orchard sitting in front of Levi and Wilma at their kitchen table.

Once pleasantries were exchanged, Carter spoke first. "I talked to the property lawyer friend of mine and he suggests doing an ownership structure called Tenancy in Common. Everyone will have a share." He passed them each a piece of paper. "This explains it a little more fully." Carter then looked at his list. "Florence, Mercy, Honor,

Joy, Hope, Favor, Cherish and Bliss will own equal shares."

"Bliss!" Wilma said. "Why take me out and include Bliss?"

Carter looked at Florence for help.

Florence said, "Bliss is part of this family now. I thought it would be nice to include her."

"It's not necessary. I think I mentioned on Monday I meant Bliss to be excluded when I mentioned the girls." Levi said, "It was a nice suggestion. You should take Bliss off."

"Are you sure?" Florence frowned.

"*Jah*. I insist upon it."

Wilma smiled. "I'm glad that's sorted. So, Florence, your brothers aren't interested?"

"No. Neither of them."

"Oh." Wilma clasped her hands together in her lap. "And how will Levi and I get money? We need to live on something."

Florence said, "We came up with the idea that the money will go into an operating account. Because you and Levi are living here, you'll be paid as caretakers and managers. Then the other accounts will be paid and whatever is left over, after some is kept in reserve, will be paid out to the individual shareholders, who are me and the girls."

"How much will we get?" asked Wilma.

"We'll have to work out the finer details. I just wanted to check with the both of you to get your opinion on the suggestion," Carter said.

"It will be enough for you to live on," added Florence. "As long as the orchard is run properly and everyone does their share of the work. Besides the apples, we'll need all the income from the apple products. That means the girls will need to be making things to sell when they're not working on the orchard."

Wilma looked over at her husband. "What do you think, Levi? You've been quiet."

Slowly, he nodded. "I think it's a sound idea."

Florence was relieved. She was hoping Levi wasn't going to see it as a handout, but he had expressed an interest in learning more. She also knew Levi had other money. Years ago, he admitted to having shares in some Amish-run businesses and they already knew he had other assets as well as the cash he often loaned to people in need.

"You've been more than fair, Florence. And Carter, thank you for finding out all this.

I'm expecting there will be fees moving forward with this."

"There will be. I'm finding that out tomorrow. My friend can do all the contract work and he won't charge me, but any transfer fees to the state, Florence and I will cover."

"That's good of you," Wilma said. "Thank you."

"Wilma and I will contribute. I insist," said Levi.

"Why don't we wait and see how much it is first?" suggested Florence. "Are you happy with that?"

"I am," said Wilma.

"Good."

"I'll tell my friend to move ahead with things, shall I?" Carter asked.

Levi nodded. "Thank you, Carter."

"Why don't you men sit in the living room near the fire? And, Florence, help me to fix us some hot tea?" Wilma stood.

"Okay."

After the men left the room, Florence stood. "It's awfully quiet. Where are the girls?"

"I told them to leave us while we discuss things." Wilma filled the teakettle with water and then placed it on the lit gas stove. She turned to face Florence who was pulling the cups and saucers out of the cupboard.

"Florence, why would you suggest Bliss have part ownership?"

"Because she's part of the family."

"I know, she is now but your *vadder* didn't even know her."

"He would've known her from the community. She was probably five when he died."

"That's not what I meant. He wouldn't have known her as a daughter. This is about what he wanted, and he wanted his family to have the orchard. I'm part of the family too."

"Do you want to be included? Because we can do that if you want. I was just thinking of the children."

Wilma huffed. "Too late. If you change it now, Levi will think that I made a fuss. He'll think I'm a dreadful person. More so than he already does."

"It's so sad."

"What is?"

"That he thinks you're a dreadful person." Florence smiled. "I'm joking. Of course he doesn't think that."

Wilma didn't say anything. She just grabbed the white china teapot from the corner of the benchtop, opened the jar and shook in some tea leaves without even bothering to measure.

Florence was certain Wilma still wasn't sorry for hiding the will. Soon, the orchard would be safe. Safe from being sold to some stranger. Florence knew her years of prayers had stopped that from happening. Her father would be happy about that.

"Everything seems to work out for you, Florence. You left the community and yet here you are back here and about to take ownership of everything."

Florence was so shocked at Wilma's words that she didn't know what to say. "Firstly, it's what *Dat* wanted. Secondly, even though it was supposed to be willed to me and me alone, I'm including your daughters. I don't know what more I can do to be fair. What would you have me do?"

"Nothing." Wilma turned around and turned off the gas before the water in the kettle had even boiled. Then she poured the lukewarm water into the teapot. "There's a tray around here somewhere. It'll make it easier to carry everything out."

"Wilma, wait."

Wilma looked at her. "Yes?"

"I can tell you're annoyed. Let's talk this through."

"I am. I'm annoyed that you left us, left this community and yet things work out well for you. The sun shines upon you no matter what you do. You always were your father's favorite. He even preferred your mother over me and even you over me, which his will backs up." She gave a sharp nod of her head. "There. I've said it."

Florence covered her mouth in shock. Her stepmother was jealous of Eleanor. "You're wrong, Wilma. *Dat* loved you. He loved my mother too, I'm sure, but he loved you as well."

Tears misted in Wilma's eyes. Florence put her arm around her. "Let's sit for a minute. They can wait for their tea." Florence guided Wilma to the kitchen table where they both sat. "I've given things a lot of thought over the last months. I realized something."

Wilma blinked away the tears. "What?"

"I think *Dat* never expected to die. He might have thought he'd outlast you because you were often so unwell. He thought he'd be old when he died and that would mean you would be old too. That's why he left it to me. He knew I loved the orchard and I would leave you and the family in the house for the rest of your lives. That's what he wanted."

Wilma sniffed. "He didn't expect to go so soon."

"That's right. He didn't."

"Is that what you truly think, Florence?"

"I know it. I could tell by the way he looked at you that he loved you. He really did and I'm not just saying it. I don't even remember my mother, but I do remember my father and you together. I'm not making up stories."

A smile lifted the corners of Wilma's lips. "That makes me feel better. It was a shock to read that will and see I was left out, forgotten, ignored as though me and even my girls were never a thought in his head."

"That's not the way it was. He loved you and the girls, you must know he did."

"I hope you're right."

"I am. You stay there, I'll finish making the tea." Florence got up and put the teakettle back on the stove, threw out the lukewarm contents of the teapot and arranged the cups, saucers, cream and sugar onto a tray.

It seemed nothing had changed in the Baker household. She was still looking after her stepmother, and not the other way around.

As soon as they finished their tea, Florence gave Carter a special look and he knew it was time to leave. Wilma had seemed better after their talk and had been all smiles when they said goodbye.

They got in the car and left to collect Iris from Christina.

As soon as their car left the driveway and turned onto the road, Carter said, "You were a long time getting the tea. I ran out of things to talk about with Levi. We ended up just sitting there looking around the room."

"She was upset she wasn't included in the ownership. I said we'd change it to include her, but then I found out she was really just upset about not being included in the will. It must've been hurtful. She felt forgotten by the man she loved."

"I guess so. I can see how she'd feel that way."

Florence sighed. "I had to talk to her for a while and convince her my father did love her. I think she's still a little jealous of my mother."

"It must be hard, though, always wondering about the first spouse when you're a second spouse."

Florence smiled. "If something happened to me, your second wife would have a lot to live up to."

"Don't even joke about it."

Florence laughed.

Carter said, "One thing is for certain, she'd have to learn about orchards, fast. Sink or swim with the apples."

"That's why you should be more involved."

"I don't know how you work that out, but no thanks. I'm involved as much as I want to be right now. I still have my businesses to run. Speaking of which, I can't wait until we're in our new home and I can spread out in my office. I'm so unorganized right now. And I've got that team meeting next week. I've got a lot to do between now and then."

"I'll miss our old cottage."

"I might too, briefly, but not for long. We're busting out at the seams." He glanced over at her and gave her a big smile that warmed her heart.

Chapter 19

That night over dinner, Levi told everyone what had been decided upon with Florence and Carter. He also told them that no one else needed to know until things were official.

Everything would change, he'd said. Florence would take over, and Cherish knew that meant there'd be no place to hide. Everyone would have to do their fair share of the work. Just as well it was winter and the work in the orchard was the lowest when the trees were dormant.

After everyone went to bed that night, Cherish heard voices coming from outside her bedroom window. In the darkness, she pushed Caramel aside and moved the quilt and crept to the window. She lifted it open a crack allowing in the cold night air. She closed her eyes against the breeze and listened.

"I hope I'm not calling too late." It was Caroline's voice.

A male voice responded, "No. I couldn't sleep."

Cherish narrowed her eyes and could just make out Caroline's shape in the moonlight, standing against a clump of trees speaking into her cellphone. And, it was on speaker and the sound carried to Cherish's ears in the stillness of the night. Cherish had clearly recognized Eddie's voice.

"I haven't heard from you lately," Caroline said.

Cherish winced, hoping Eddie would stay strong.

"I'm sorry. I've been busy."

"Busy going to Cherish's café?"

"Oh, that's right. I did."

"So, would you be too busy if I change my mind about having coffee with you?" Caroline asked.

There was a long hesitation. Even Cherish didn't know what he should say. If he said no, Caroline might forget him. If he said yes, it would be too easy for her.

"I've got to go. I have another call coming through. I'll call you back, okay?"

"Yes. Wait … when?"

Then he ended the call.

Cherish couldn't believe how perfect that was. Caroline was left up in the air and left wondering who would be calling him so late. The mystery woman, of course. And, when would he call her back? Tonight, tomorrow, next week?

Caroline stood still for a while and then she lit a cigarette. After a few puffs, she sat on the cold ground. The owl that had decided to live near the barn, hooted. Caroline scrambled to her feet and quickly walked to the house.

Cherish shook with silent laughter, holding her hand over her mouth. Then the owl hooted again, causing Caroline to run. When Caroline was out of sight, Cherish closed her window and then got back into the warmth of her bed.

Tomorrow, she'd have to call Eddie and they'd work out his next move. It had to involve him bumping into Caroline, accidentally on purpose.

Cherish stretched her hand down and patted Caramel.

It was Saturday morning when Cherish called Eddie's cellphone to find out if he had a plan for the next step with Caroline.

Standing in the barn, she'd dialed his cellphone number and was waiting for him to answer.

"It's Cherish," she said when she heard him speak.

"I'm glad you called. You'll never guess—"

"Caroline called you last night."

"Yes and … How did you know?"

"I heard everything. I overheard, I should say. That's why I'm calling you now. You'll have to come here in a few days, say ... Monday. Today is too soon and we have our meeting tomorrow. When you come here, say your father sent you with more honey. Do you have some jars to spare?"

"Always."

"Come to the house at twelve thirty. I'll arrange for Caroline to be having lunch in the kitchen at that time."

"What will I do? What will I say?"

"It's a hard one. I'll give it some thought. You didn't call her back yet, did you?"

"No. I wasn't sure what to do, so I thought it was best to do nothing."

"Good. Very good work."

"So, what's the plan? I need one and I have to know what it is before I get there. I need to prepare."

Cherish giggled. "I guess you can mention taking her out for coffee, but wait until just before you leave. See if she mentions it first."

"I can do that."

"Good."

"Thanks, Cherish. I couldn't do this without you."

Cherish was pleased someone was thankful for her help, as she brushed off a smattering of dust on the phone. "We're not there yet. You need to be boyfriend and girlfriend. Just don't be too eager. She needs to think you have options other than her. Act like you're a wanted man."

"Like a criminal?"

"No!"

He laughed. "I'm just joking."

"Oh. Good. We'll talk later." Cherish hung up the phone's receiver. Then she looked down at the address book and flipped through to find Daniel's phone number.

Her hand went back on the phone as she wondered if she should call him, and then she changed her mind.

After she closed the book, she walked out of the barn feeling good about herself. It was nice to be able to help a person like Eddie. Where would he be without her? Most likely living with his ma and pa forever and a day.

Chapter 20

After the early morning meeting on Sunday, Cherish sat down with Joy and Hope to eat the meal at the bishop's house. The bishop had the perfect set-up at his place for hosting gatherings in the cold weather with rows of tables under cover. The structure was closed on three sides and one open wall faced the house.

Hope sat between her two sisters. "This is embarrassing. Everyone will notice we're not together. We always eat together and talk to each other. Now we're eating separately and we're nowhere near one another."

Cherish glanced to where Hope was staring. She wasn't surprised when she saw her sister had been looking at Fairfax.

"You're not getting along with Fairfax. *Mamm's* not getting along with Ada. What's happening in the world? It's turned upside down."

"Don't be dramatic all the time," Joy told Cherish. Joy had always been the sensible one of the family, old beyond her years.

"It's okay for you, Joy," Hope almost snapped. "Look how things have turned out for you."

Cherish was a little shocked to hear Hope speak like that to Joy.

A veil of sadness covered Joy's pretty face. "Well, things aren't perfect."

Was there something happening that Cherish wasn't aware of? "Why, what's going on?"

"Oh, nothing." Joy looked down.

Cherish could tell something was wrong and looked around for Isaac, wondering if they'd had an argument too. She finally saw him at the food table, filling his plate. He'd always been a big eater. "If there is something wrong, you should tell us."

It seemed Hope wasn't so wrapped up in her own problems that she didn't notice Joy seemed down. "I'm sorry for what I said, Joy. I'm happy for you. I truly am. It's just that I want to be as happy as you are right now and I thought I would be. I feel so selfish right now. Tell us what's going on."

Joy shook her head. "It's nothing. I'm feeling so tired, that's all. Too tired to get out of bed some days. I can't wait until the *boppli* comes and then everything can get back to normal. The *haus* is nearly fixed too. We've been able to stay in the bedroom these past weeks."

"That's good news." Cherish felt bad for not inquiring sooner about the house renovations. She had been too busy with other things and Levi's sudden illness had shaken everyone. "Isaac is a good worker."

"He certainly is. He's been working at the saddlers and coming home and doing more work in the evening on the house."

Cherish stared at Joy's face trying to work out what the problem was if it wasn't Isaac. "Do you miss all of us and your old home?"

Joy smiled. *"Nee.* I do in a way, sometimes, but mostly I enjoy the quiet and having our own home."

"Good." Hope said.

"Joy, what did you mean about things not being perfect?"

"Nothing. I shouldn't have said anything."

"Is the *boppli* okay?" asked Hope.

"Yeah, fine. Things are as perfect as they can be. That's all I meant." Joy smiled, but Cherish wondered if there was something behind that smile. At least the baby was okay, and she had said everything was fine with Isaac.

Cherish looked at Caroline who was sitting at a different table with Favor. The two of them were alone again. Hopefully, soon Caroline would be spending a lot of time with Eddie and she'd have Favor back again. That was the plan.

Isaac then sat down with them. "How are you girls today?"

"We're fine," Hope said. "We've just been hearing how well the *haus* is coming along."

"It is. We love the place now, don't we, Joy?" Isaac commented.

Joy smiled. "We do."

Isaac continued, "You girls should come and see it soon. You haven't visited in a while unless you've been there while I've been at work and Joy hasn't mentioned it. But she's been forgetful lately."

"We haven't. We have a lot of pressure on us now to work in the orchard. I'm only doing one shift at the café. One shift doesn't bring a lot of money in, but I do enjoy it. I love talking with different people. *Mamm* says I just love talking and that's probably right."

"Just stop by any time you like," Joy told the girls.

"Bliss and I were going there the other day. Um, now what day was that?" Cherish looked upward. "It was Sunday, that's right. A week ago today. We saw you had someone there already—"

"Who was there?" Joy asked.

"Bliss thought it was Hope and Fairfax, but I knew it wasn't the Millers' horse. No wait, maybe Bliss was the one who said that. I don't even know the Millers' horses."

Hope laughed. "I can't believe you don't know if you said something. It makes sense that Bliss said it. She knows horses."

"That's right. So when we saw a horse and buggy, we didn't want to interrupt, so we ended up visiting Carter and Florence. We got to hold Iris. She's just so adorable now she's that much older. When Florence talks, Iris turns her head looking for her mother. It's so cute."

"You should've taken me," Hope said.

"You were waiting for Fairfax when we left."

"Oh, that's right. We did have a nice afternoon too." Hope smiled doing a good job of covering up the problems she was having with Fairfax.

Because of the cold night, the singing was canceled and everyone went their separate ways.

All Fairfax did was nod a goodbye at Hope when they caught each other's eye as they were heading to their buggies.

After dinner, Hope was so upset that she went to bed and had an early night, but not before praying that Fairfax would sort out all his problems quickly.

Chapter 21

The next day, everyone was nearly finished with breakfast when they heard a car. Wilma looked out the window and was soon joined by Caroline.

"It's Eddie!" Caroline wasn't able to hold back her excitement.

"The beekeeper's son?" asked Wilma.

"I wonder why he's here." Cherish couldn't help but smile.

"I don't know." Wilma threw her hands in the air. "Will he come in for coffee or something? I need to know before I do a final clean."

"I'll find out." Cherish got up from the table.

"I can do that." Caroline moved in front of her. "You stay here, Cherish."

"Okay." Cherish sat back down and her mother walked over to her.

"Why are you letting her answer the door? He's not here to see Caroline. He's here to see one of us."

"*Mamm,* I think he might be here to see Caroline." Cherish gave her mother a wink.

Wilma's jaw dropped open and then she covered her mouth and laughed. "I didn't know."

"Neither do I, officially. It's just a good guess." Cherish left the table and walked to the doorway to listen.

"Don't do that," Wilma whispered, moving up close behind her.

"Please let me. I don't have much entertainment in life."

Wilma shrugged and turned back to the sink. "Well, if he's not coming in here I'm going to make sandwiches for Florence and Levi. They've been in the orchard since sunup and they must be freezing by now. I'll toast the sandwiches and you can take them a thermos of hot tea too."

"Fine."

When Caroline opened the door, Eddie found it difficult to act uninterested in her. She was so beautiful. Her creamy skin was a perfect match with her long spirals of light-colored hair that framed her perfect oval face. She also seemed pleased to see him judging by the smile on her plumped-up lips.

"Hello, Eddie."

"Oh, what a surprise. I forgot for a moment that you were staying here. You're still here I see?"

She frowned and the smile instantly left her face. "I was just talking to you on the phone a few days ago."

"That's right. I remember that now." He looked down at the honey, desperately trying to remember all Cherish's instructions. "I brought some honey for the household. My father asked me to bring it here."

She looked down at the box. "That's very nice, but we still have plenty."

"No matter. Shall I bring it in?"

"No. I'll take it."

He passed the box over. "Thanks ... Caroline, isn't it?"

"You forgot my name?"

He wasn't sure if that was a good move or not. He'd made that name-forgetting idea up by himself. "No. I just meant ... I wondered if you ever went by the name Carol."

"Never. That's like a totally different name. People with my name rarely shorten it to Carol. It's either Caroline or Carrie, but not Carol."

"I see. I didn't mean to offend you."

"You didn't."

"Are you sure? I should make it up to you somehow." He bit his lip.

273

The corners of her lips tilted upward. "We could go for that coffee."

"That's right. I remember now, I invited you for coffee a while back."

"You did and I'm up for it. Unless ... there's a certain reason you can't?"

He chuckled. "No. There's no reason at all. When should we do this?" He rubbed the back of his neck. "Perhaps tomorrow, early afternoon?"

"Sure. I think I'll be able to get away, being a Tuesday tomorrow."

"Wait. I forgot tomorrow is Tuesday. Just a minute." He needed to act like he had other options. He pulled out his cellphone and looked at it, scrolled through it. Then he placed it back in his pocket. "I'll have to juggle some things around, but I can do that. Shall I collect you, at say ... two?"

"That would be great and then no one would have to drive me anywhere. The buggies are so slow. It gets frustrating when you need to get somewhere in a hurry."

"I'll see you tomorrow at around two, give or take."

"I'll be waiting."

He gave her a nod and then turned around and headed to his car, pleased that he'd gotten through it, and successfully. Cherish would be pleased with him. Now he just had to hope that things worked out well tomorrow.

When Eddie drove away, Caroline closed the door and headed into the kitchen with the honey. She was met by Wilma and Cherish, both standing there staring at her.

"Who was that?" Wilma asked.

"Eddie. Just like I said. He brought us all this honey." She glanced at the box in her arms.

"Ah, that was so good of him."

"More honey?" Wilma smiled.

"I know. We have a lot now."

"I think he came here because he's fond of you, Caroline," Wilma said.

Caroline placed the box of honey on the countertop. "We are having coffee tomorrow afternoon, if I can leave here for a couple of hours."

"Of course." Wilma nodded.

"Cherish said she saw him with another woman. If he really liked me, he wouldn't have been out with someone else. Is that true what you said, Cherish?"

"What reason would I have to lie about it? I can't believe you're doubting me."

"It could've been his sister," Wilma said.

"He is an only child," Cherish said, "but it could've been his cousin."

"Cherish, you said they were cozying up together."

"I did, that's what it seemed like, but I could've been wrong."

"You're both trying to make me feel better."

"So, you do like him?" Wilma asked.

"I'm not sure yet. I do want to get to know him better. That's all I know for now. I think he had something else he was going to do tomorrow and that was probably doing something with a woman. He should be totally focused on me, if he likes me."

Cherish said, "Maybe after tomorrow he will be. It sounds like you'll have to make a big effort to make him like you."

"We'll see. Where does the honey go, Mrs. Bruner?"

"Just leave it. I'll put it away."

"I better go back to the shop." Caroline left the room.

"That would be nice if she married the beekeeper's son. The bees are so important to the orchard. I might not know much about the trees, but I do know that much. If we didn't have our neighbors keeping bees, we would need our own hives."

Cherish grimaced. "I don't like the sound of that. I don't know the first thing ... Well, that's not exactly right. I do know a little bit since Eddie showed us around that day."

"We're struggling to do things already. Oh, I was making toasted sandwiches to take to Florence and Levi."

"Why don't you put the honey away and I'll finish off the sandwiches. I'll even go out and find them."

"Okay."

Chapter 22

Cherish took the sandwiches, covered with a tea-towel, into the orchard on a plate. Tucked under her arm was a large thermos that she'd filled with hot coffee.

Florence had told her they'd be working on the trees down near the fence line that divided her property from theirs.

For the first time, it occurred to Cherish that her father would've been pleased that the part of the property he had to sell had come back into the family. The orchard had been through a tough time due to years of unseasonable weather. He'd had to sell off a portion of land that wasn't good for planting because it was low-lying. On a high area of that land was a cottage and a couple of smaller, old stone buildings that had since been destroyed. Carter had bought that same land from the original people her father had sold it to.

"Go find them, Caramel," she said to her dog.

He just looked up at her and continued walking by her side.

"Florence and Levi. Find them. Go!"

Caramel barked at her and then leaped in bounds beside her.

"You'll never be one of those search and rescue dogs." A little further along, she came across them. Levi was sitting in a fold-up chair while Florence was showing him how to prune.

"Lunch!" Cherish called out.

Levi twisted to look at her and Florence looked up.

"Carter has already brought us food," Florence told her.

"And we've eaten it already."

"Oh, we didn't know. *Mamm* went to a lot of trouble toasting sandwiches."

Levi leaned over looking at the wrapped bundle. "What's on those?"

"Never you mind, Levi. You're not supposed to eat a lot at one time."

He looked a little taken aback. "I'm out of the danger zone now."

"*Nee.* Little and often is how you're supposed to eat."

He chuckled. "Often is the part I like to remember from that comment. Not so sure about the 'little' part."

"You can have a snack later. What about coffee?"

"No, thanks, Cherish. We've just had green tea."

"Oh, green tea?"

"It was different, but nice," Levi told her.

"Okay then. I'll take these back to the house. Are you two having fun?"

"I think so," Florence said. "Tell me you know how to prune, don't you? You were shown often enough."

"*Jah,* sure. I'd lose that one there." Cherish pointed to a branch growing off to one side. "And those knobbly bits underneath it."

"Good."

"I'm naturally good at a lot of things. I've been good at everything I've tried so far. The people at the café love me. That means I'm a good worker there too."

"I'm not happy about the café and you still working there."

Cherish made a face. She shouldn't have mentioned the café. "It helps me get away and just be myself. It's hard being home all the time with the same people. I do like to get out and as I said before, it acts as my free time."

"Well, you better stop nattering, go back to the house and do something useful," Levi told her.

"Okay. Come on, Caramel."

"Cherish, before you go, I was just telling Levi that normally we wouldn't prune now, being the beginning of winter, because it will stimulate growth and we don't want the trees growing in the winter. We want new growth in the spring, so it's best to prune in late winter. It's just that... it hasn't been done properly for the last few seasons. Did you prune the trees at all last year, Cherish, or, has anyone?"

"Not that I can remember." She could tell Florence was disappointed in her, but the workload was daunting. No one had shown interest in the orchard. She wasn't the only one.

"Just wondering. It seems all the trees haven't been pruned or if they have, they haven't been pruned well."

"I'll go back to the *haus* and help *Mamm*. Are you warm enough, Levi? You don't want to catch a cold. Shall I bring you an extra blanket?"

"I'm warm enough under all these layers, *denke*."

"Okay, bye." Cherish turned away and walked back. Once she was out of sight, she ate two toasted corned beef and pickle sandwiches and then she gave the last one to Caramel. When she got back to the house, no one was home.

It was unusually quiet.

She washed up the plate and then left it to dry on the rack beside the sink, and left the flask of coffee on the countertop. Someone could drink that later.

Cherish figured her mother was helping the girls in the shop at the front of their property near the road. She saw that her mother had left off peeling apples so she sat down and continued that task.

As she did the monotonous job of peeling, she thought some more about Fairfax and

Hope. She'd been able to distract Caroline so she wouldn't be chasing Fairfax at his most vulnerable, but how could she fix things between Fairfax and Hope? It was eating away at her that she'd made things worse.

There had to be something she could do. Perhaps if he thought Hope was sick, or missing, or possibly dying, then his true feelings would surface.

No. She made a face and shook her head. If she did anything like that people would find out and she'd be in all kinds of trouble.

Or maybe ... what if Fairfax thought there was a chance of losing Hope to someone else? It seemed to be working with Caroline and Eddie. But how would she do that? Who could Hope like besides Fairfax?

No. Hope would never agree to anything like that. She was already upset with her for interfering and there was always a chance of making things even worse than they were now.

Cherish heard the front door open and then close. Wilma walked into the kitchen and placed a letter down in front of her. Cherish looked up at her. "For me?"

"*Jah.*"

"My hands are too juicy from these apples to look on the back. Did you see who it was from?"

Wilma smirked. "Can't you tell from the writing by now? He writes you all the time."

Cherish stared at the envelope. The writing was barely legible. "Oh, it's from Malachi."

"*Jah.* Isn't this your weekly letter?"

"He's written three or four times now without me even having a chance to write back."

Wilma tsk-tsked. "Cherish. It doesn't take long to sit down and write something."

"I guess so. I'll write to him tonight."

"See that you do."

"I will, and I'll post it next time I'm in town. I hope he's working hard enough and not spending all his time writing."

"He's probably lonely, isolated on the farm. It's a long distance from anywhere."

"There are a few things around. A few shops. A post office, and then there's Ruth next door."

"Still, it's not the same as living here. I do wish you'd reconsider moving there."

"Never." Cherish looked down at the last apple on the table. "What are we making?"

"Apple pies."

"Good. My favorite." Wilma got the flour out and started putting it through the sifter. *"Mamm,* how did you know you were in love with *Dat?"*

"Ah, he was a very kind man. He was widowed with three adorable *kinner,* and my *mudder* said to me he'd look after me."

"Oh, so my *grossmammi* matched you together?"

"Not exactly. It wasn't like that. I had to wait a few years for him to even talk to me. I was so happy when he sought me out at every meeting or gatherings. Things went from there. He needed help with the *kinner,* mostly Florence, when he was in the orchard and I often came here and helped out."

"Sounds romantic."

Wilma frowned at her. "It was for me. It might not sound that way, but I was very much in love with him."

"And, I know he was in love with you too. I remember how it was with the two of you. It must be a nice feeling to have someone love you. For someone to choose you above every other woman they know and every other woman that they might meet in their future."

"I've been blessed that way twice."

Cherish reached for a hand towel that was at the end of the table and wiped her hands. Then she studied Wilma's face. Was she really in love with Levi or had it been a marriage of convenience? Someone to work on the orchard and do other tasks that Wilma was too lazy to do for herself? Things had been in such a mess when Florence walked out on them. Wilma didn't know a thing about the orchard and

Florence had always run the household and the finances from as far back as Cherish could remember.

Cherish didn't have to wonder too hard which husband Wilma liked best. It was her father. He had been the love of her mother's life. But everyone had grown used to Levi and his strange ways.

Underneath Levi's gruff surface, he seemed to have a good heart.

"What do you think of Bliss and Adam? Do you think they're a good match?"

Wilma looked up from over the mountain of flour. *"Jah,* don't you?"

"Jah. Well, what about Fairfax and Hope?"

"I think they're a good match too. A little young, but all my girls are marrying young it seems."

"Hmm."

"Do you like one of them? Want one of those men for yourself. Is that where this is headed?"

"*Nee.* I'm just trying to figure out a few things."

"Cherish, I don't know if anyone's ever told you this, but you don't have to talk all the time. Can we have a quiet moment? Or some quiet moments? Sometimes I don't want to talk and your constant questions make things impossible."

"Sorry."

"That's okay."

"It won't happen again."

"Good." Wilma looked up at her. "Now that you've finished peeling the apples, we need the inside and the outside of the windows cleaned."

"Windows again? We only did them last week. They look fine."

"That's right, windows again, if you want to look out of them. Otherwise, we can let them get black and we won't need to use the curtains." Wilma chortled at what she just said.

"Sounds good to me." Cherish got up from the table. "Okay. I'm going. Inside and the outside."

"*Jah,* and start with the ones outside."

Cherish went to the mudroom and filled the bucket with the glass cleaning mixture and water, and headed around to start with the windows under the cover of the porch.

When she finally made her move to the farm, she'd only clean the things that needed cleaning. She wouldn't clean imaginary dirt off things. Cherish suspected her mother wanted to be rid of her and get some peace.

While she scrubbed the first window, she remembered she'd left the letter from Malachi on the kitchen table.

Chapter 23

When her task of window cleaning was done, Cherish grabbed Malachi's letter from the kitchen table and hurried to her room.

Sprawled on her bed, she opened it. As usual it took her some time to work out what he meant to tell her. His writing was so bad. Again, he asked her when she was coming back to the farm and, again, he said he missed their talks.

Nothing at all about how the farm was doing, or any of the livestock, and Cherish found that annoying. She threw the letter down on the bed. She had enough friends. She didn't need to make a friend out of Malachi. He was simply there to do a job, to look after her farm until she could get back there to stay.

She pulled a sheet of paper out of the box of note paper she'd gotten for Christmas and pulled out a pen from the same box. Then she sat back on her bed and reached for her Bible to put the paper on as she wrote.

Dear Malachi,

Why haven't you told me anything about the farm? All I've asked you for is an update once in a while. Is that too hard to do?

She stopped, looked at what she'd written and then ripped it up. She couldn't write that. It sounded too mean. She needed a straightforward approach that was also kind.

Dear Malachi ...

Hope burst into her room. "What are you doing?"

"Writing a letter to Malachi."

Hope sat down on the bed. It was obvious she wanted to talk. "What are you writing to him about?"

"He keeps writing to me and not saying anything. Nothing about the farm."

"Oh, that would be frustrating and you're so far away with no idea what is going on."

"What should I say to him? I've already made one attempt, but I sounded too mean. You know how I can be abrupt when I don't want to be that way."

"When are you posting your letter?"

"Tomorrow. I'll take it in to town. Can you tell me what to write?"

"Maybe I should write a letter to Fairfax."

Cherish stared at her sister, wondering if she'd heard right. "Why? You can go right over and talk to him anytime you want."

"I know, but I'm thinking in a letter I can put my thoughts together better. I can tell him how I really feel deep down. Get everything out into the open."

"I don't know."

"Well, you're not old enough to know what it's like to be in a relationship and try to communicate with someone. Sometimes I feel like I'm not heard. If I write the words, he'll have to be quiet and read them."

Cherish shrugged. "If you want. What would you say?"

"I'll have to give it some thought. If I write it tonight, will you be able to post it for me tomorrow?"

"Sure, but I'd give it a lot of thought. Don't say any angry words."

"I won't."

"Good."

Hope jumped to her feet and went to walk out the door, but Cherish stopped her.

"Hey, you're supposed to be helping me write this letter. What will I say?"

"Whatever you want to say."

Cherish groaned. "Unfair."

Hope spied Cherish's writing paper. "Can I borrow a page?"

"Sure take a couple."

"I think I'll only need one. *Denke.*" Hope grabbed a piece of notepaper and disappeared out the door.

Cherish settled back down and wrote the nicest letter she could. She thanked him for the good job he was doing and asked him to send another letter, this time telling her exactly what was going on with the farm. At the end of the letter, she told him that it was going to be hard for her to get away and it looked like she wouldn't be able to get there until the warmer weather. She signed her name, folded the letter in three and popped it in an envelope.

Once it was addressed and sealed, she was relieved. It was a load off her shoulders. Now, she just had to remember to post it.

Cherish placed everything carefully back in her box, and then she placed the sealed letter on her tall chest of drawers in clear view.

She switched off the gas lamp on her bedside table and then pulled the quilt over herself.

Caramel pushed her bedroom door open with his nose, and inched his way inside.

"Up you get."

Caramel jumped onto the end of the bed and turned around twice before he lay down making himself comfortable.

Chapter 24

The next day, Bliss and Cherish headed into town to collect some supplies. Cherish had the two letters in her hands. She held Hope's letter to Fairfax up in the air and noticed it wasn't sealed properly. It was a temptation too great to resist. While Bliss was talking about something, Cherish commented yes and no in the right places and set about opening the envelope. Then she unfolded the letter and read it.

As she suspected, it was bad and she was pleased she'd opened it.

"This is dreadful, Bliss. Hope can't say this."

Bliss gasped when she saw the letter in Cherish's hand. "You've opened her letter?"

"Jah, I did, and I'm not sorry. She says, *if that's all you think of me then we shouldn't be together."*

"Oh no. She can't be serious. This will upset him for certain."

"I know. What do you think? Should I send it?"

"You should because she asked you to. Also, you shouldn't have read it in the first place."

"I can't send it. No, I can't." She held it in the air. "I'm going to go back and confess what I've done. I'll tell her that I've read it and I'll tell her she mustn't send it. It would break my heart if the two of them don't end up married. They had the perfect romance, the perfect love."

"That's a good idea, to confess what you did."

"Good. I'm glad you agree."

For the rest of the day, Cherish could think about nothing else. Hope had to see sense.

When they got home a few hours later, Cherish found Hope in the house just starting to wash the stairs.

Cherish stood at the bottom of the stairway and held the letter out. "You can't write this."

Hope looked down at her. "Is that my letter?"

"*Jah.*"

"Why didn't you post it? Wait. Did you read it?"

"Jah."

"I thought I could trust you. I thought you'd learned your lesson from the Bliss letter thing."

"I did. I could've written a better letter for you, one much better than this, but I didn't." Cherish took another step toward Hope, waving the envelope in the air. "This will break you two apart."

"Nee, it won't."

Cherish marched up the stairs and faced Hope on the top step. "It's a bad idea to send this. I know I shouldn't have read it, but it's just as well I did."

"You're right. Thanks for not sending it. I just want him to know how I feel. If he can't handle that, then maybe we aren't meant for each other. A relationship should be a two-way thing."

"And it is, but don't wreck it."

"Lately, it's been all his way. All his timing. What about my timing? What about what I want? Everyone is tiptoeing around him because he's new in the community, but guess what, he's a grown man."

"Are you talking about me?"

Both Hope and Cherish swung around. Fairfax was right there standing at the bottom of the stairs and Wilma stood rigidly beside him.

Chapter 25

Cherish couldn't believe that Fairfax had overheard what Hope said. It wasn't exactly mean, but it wasn't nice either.

Wilma said, "Fairfax drove me home. The horse was lame. Fairfax's friend, Matt, is walking the beast home."

"'The beast?'" Cherish asked.

"The horse."

"Oh. That's nice of you, Fairfax," Cherish said. "Where were you heading, *Mamm?*"

"Just out to talk with Ada. I didn't get far."

"Were you talking about me just now, Hope?" Fairfax asked.

Cherish didn't want to be around when they talked, so she ran down the stairs. *"Mamm,* I've got something outside I've been meaning to show you."

"What is it?"

"The windows. I want to show you how clean they are." Cherish grabbed her mother and started walking with her, and they didn't stop until they were out the front door and standing on the porch.

"Why are you pulling on my arm?" *Mamm* pulled away from her.

Cherish let go. "I thought we should give them some privacy so they can talk."

"They see each other every second day, what could they possibly have to talk about?"

Cherish stared at her mother. Why couldn't she see what was going on around her? "Couldn't you tell things were frosty just now?"

"Between the two of them?"

"*Jah.*"

"*Nee.* Not really. Hope said he was a grown man. That's all I heard."

Cherish sighed. "Don't worry, *Mamm.*"

Wilma walked over and looked at the windows. "It's an okay job, but not a great one." She turned around to look at Cherish. "Why was this so important to show me?"

Cherish flopped into one of the two porch chairs. "Don't worry, *Mamm.*"

"Is that your latest saying now? You drag me out here into the cold and worry me about Fairfax and Hope and then you tell me not to worry."

"*Jah,* that's right. Don't worry."

"I'll never understand you, Cherish." Wilma's teeth chattered with the cold. Neither of them had taken time to grab a coat on their way out.

"That makes two of us."

Back inside, Hope felt awful about being overheard. She joined Fairfax at the bottom of the stairs. "What are you doing here? I thought you needed time."

"I brought your *mudder* home, back to her *haus.*"

She smiled when she heard him speaking some words of Pennsylvania Dutch. She'd asked him to practice it and he was. "Shall we sit somewhere?"

"*Jah.* Sure. Let's go into the kitchen. Everyone's out."

They walked to the kitchen in awkward silence and once there, Fairfax pulled a chair out for her and then sat down next to her.

"Can I get you a hot drink? Or maybe some soup?"

"No." He looked up at the ceiling and then scratched his neck. "This is probably all my fault. I did say we'd get married as soon as we could, but I didn't literally mean the very minute I converted."

She was glad he was talking calmly. Maybe they could make progress. "Oh. I thought you did."

"*Nee*. We will be married, if you still want me."

She leaned forward. It was what she'd been waiting to hear. She thought she'd lost him. "I do." Waiting was the last thing she wanted. How long would she have to wait? That's the only thing she wanted to ask him, but she didn't want to make him upset or pressure him further. He'd made the biggest adjustment in his life, for her and for *Gott*.

"I need to sort a few things out and then when everything is right, we'll take the next step."

She nodded. What else could she do? Everything was going to be in Fairfax's timing. And because he didn't want to marry her right now, she couldn't help feeling rejected. "That's fine," she managed to say.

"Good. I'm glad we got that out of the way. Now, I don't need any more time. Things can go back to normal."

She stood up. "You might not, but I might take my turn to have a few days so I can think things through." She moved past him and he bounded to his feet.

"A few days to do what?" he asked.

She turned around to face him. "A few days to think things through."

"We don't need to take it turnabout, Hope."

"Do you mind if you see yourself out?" She didn't wait for his answer, and continued up the stairs to her bedroom. Then she closed the door.

Wilma and Cherish were huddled together on the cold porch. "She's just gone up to her room," Cherish said, with her nose pressed on the window.

"How do you know?"

"I just saw her."

"By herself?" Wilma asked.

"Jah, she'd hardly go to her room with Fairfax. That wouldn't be allowed, would it? Or would it?"

"Don't be silly, Cherish. I just meant, if she's in her room, where's Fairfax? Did she leave him alone in the kitchen?"

"Here he comes. Quick. Sit down and act normal."

Wilma and Cherish were sitting in the porch chairs by the time Fairfax opened the front door and stepped out. He was drained of color. Cherish knew they'd had another disagreement.

He forced a smile when he saw them. "Bye, Cherish. Bye, Mrs. Bruner."

"Thank you once again for bringing me home."

He smiled. "No sign of Matt?"

Cherish rose to her feet and then walked to the edge of the porch and looked down the road. "No sign yet."

"I'll see if I can find where he's at."

"Denke," Wilma said.

Cherish followed Fairfax to his buggy determined to find out what was going on between him and Hope. "Is everything okay? You look a little stressed."

He stopped walking. "Everything is fine. Just fine. You're not stirring up trouble, are you?"

Cherish's mouth dropped open. *"Nee!* What trouble?"

"Between me and Hope."

"*Nee.* You know me better than that. All I want is for you both to be happy. That's why I visited you."

"I don't like the way she's acting. I didn't know she had a stubborn streak. Just as well I found out now." He pushed his hat further onto his head and kept walking to his buggy.

Cherish was offended. When she walked back to the porch, Wilma called out, "What did you ask him?"

So Hope wouldn't overhear, Cherish hurried to sit down next to her. "I just said I hoped there wasn't any problem. He said there was none."

"He looked a little odd. Something's wrong. Whatever it is, you must allow them to work it out for themselves."

"I will."

"Will you?"

She saw Wilma was staring at her. "I just said I would."

"I've come to realize that what you say and what you mean are often two entirely different things."

"That's not fair, *Mamm.*"

Wilma chuckled. "I don't think you have a mean bone in your body, Cherish. It's just that you don't think about things the way everyone else does."

"Denke, Mamm. I'll take that as a compliment."

"It wasn't meant to be one."

"No matter. So, what's happening between you and Ada. Are you friends again?"

"We always have been."

"I'm not stupid, *Mamm*. I know something's going on. Ada hasn't been here for days."

"Ada is a little upset that she wasn't involved with a big decision. That's all."

"I know. I was the one who had to uninvite her, remember? Bliss and I were, I should say. She wasn't happy at all."

"She'll come around. Everyone calms down from things and then life goes on. People forget and forgive."

Cherish shivered when the wind whistled under the arches of the porch. "Why are we still out here in the cold?"

Wilma reached out her hands. "Help me up and we can warm ourselves by the fire."

Cherish hesitated. "What about the horse that's lame?"

"Bliss can treat the beast when it gets here."

"Aw, *Mamm*. Don't call the poor animal a beast. He's obviously in pain and needs tender loving care."

"It is a beast. I needed to see Ada to talk and it wouldn't co-operate. Anyway, Bliss is good with horses and she's a caring soul. She'll nurse the beast back to health and happiness."

Cherish sighed. Her mother's attitude was so cold and uncaring, but she would never change. *Mamm* didn't like any animals at all. Not their dogs, not their barn cats, not their horses, and especially not Timmy, the blue budgerigar.

Cherish jumped to her feet, took her mother by the arm and pulled her to her feet.

Together they walked into the house.

Chapter 26

The next day, Cherish realized she couldn't do anything to help Hope. She was glad that at least Hope had thanked her for not sending the letter.

Now, what was wrong with Joy?

She hadn't been herself, and Isaac had also seemed odd on Sunday. Maybe it was the wintertime and people were too cooped up inside their houses, causing them to act weirdly. She asked Hope to drive her to Joy's.

As the horse and buggy rounded a corner, the small house that Joy and Isaac lived in came into view.

"I feel like I haven't talked to her in ages."

"I know, but don't come in now. Come in when you collect me."

"Oh. I thought we were both visiting her."

"I have something to discuss in private with Joy."

"Why didn't you tell me that before?"

Cherish shrugged. "I thought I did."

"*Nee*. Why don't you tell me your problems?"

"I might. I just want to see what Joy says first. Is that all right?"

Finally, Hope nodded. "I guess it's good you're talking about them with someone.

What am I supposed to do for half an hour?"

"Drive past the dairy and see if you can see Fairfax."

"*Nee*. I will not."

"I don't know, then."

Hope grumbled. "I'll get a coffee from the general store up the road. Or, I might just go home."

"Good idea. I'll owe you a favor."

"Just one?"

Cherish giggled. "A lot of favors, then."

When Hope pulled the buggy up outside the house, Cherish ran to the door and knocked on it. When Joy answered it, she turned around and waved to Hope.

Joy stepped back to let her in. "This is a surprise. Who dropped you off?"

"Hope, but she's coming back in about a half hour. Isaac's not home, is he?"

"*Nee*, he's at work. Do you want hot tea?"

"I'll have a mint tea if you have it."

"Sure."

Minutes later, they sat down to drink tea at the small round table to one side of the living room. Cherish dunked her cookie in the tea and then took a bite. When she swallowed, she summoned up some courage to talk. "What's going on, Joy? I know something is. You're not yourself. If it's not the *boppli* or a problem with Isaac, what is it?"

"I don't know what you're talking about. I'm fine."

"That's not true. I know there's something bothering you. Is it this *haus*?" Cherish looked around.

"What's wrong with it?"

"Nothing. It's beautiful with what you've done with it." She saw the corners of Joy's lips turn downward. "If you tell me what the problem is, I can help."

"What problem could I have? Everything is going so well and my *boppli* will be in my arms in just ten weeks. I can hardly wait for the day. Neither can Isaac. We'll be a family."

"I know, but you just look so sad. Not your usual self at all." Cherish moved in the hard wooden chair to get more comfortable. "You've normally got all the answers. You're always quoting scriptures before you tell people what to do, or what you think they should be doing."

"And?"

"And you haven't done that for ages."

Joy measured out two spoonfuls of sugar and stirred them into her tea. "You haven't visited me for weeks, so how would you know?"

"Sorry about that. I've been busy with the orchard and watching over Levi, keeping the house running and all that stuff. The shop's closing next week for the wintertime, so I'll have more time. Caroline and Favor are in the shop today."

Joy nodded.

"So, tell me. What's going on?"

Joy shook her head and Cherish noticed tears welling in her sister's eyes.

"It's too shameful. It's too shameful to tell you, or to tell anyone."

That confirmed she'd been right. There was something going on with Joy. "You'll feel better if you tell me. A problem shared is a problem halved."

"I did something dreadful. You'll hate me if I tell you, but I feel ... I need to tell someone."

Cherish stared at her older sister. Joy was always the upstanding one in the family. She was the one everyone looked up to. "It can't be that bad."

"I stole something. There, I said it."

No. She couldn't have heard right. Joy would never do anything like that. "Deliberately?"

"Jah." Joy burst into tears and sobbed into her hands.

Cherish was deeply upset. How could her sister do something so awful? It wasn't in her nature to even think of taking something that didn't belong to her. It was confusing. Looking at Joy crying, Cherish felt awful for her. Cherish moved off her chair and put her arms around Joy. "Everyone does bad things. No one is perfect. *Gott* forgives us."

"Now I hate myself. Isaac looks at me differently."

"Isaac knows?"

Joy nodded.

Then Cherish remembered the odd comment that Isaac had made on Sunday about Joy. Cherish handed her a paper napkin and Joy wiped her eyes and face.

"Denke." And then she blew her nose.

Cherish tried to hide how shocked she was by her sister's admission. How could Joy steal anything? If someone else had told her Joy had done that, she never would've believed them. "What did you steal?"

"A baby dress."

"Why?" Cherish was still in disbelief.

"It was pretty."

Cherish wanted to get to the bottom of the whole thing. "But why?"

Joy sighed. "Isaac has me on a strict budget. I can barely get enough for food and there's nothing over."

"Nothing left over?"

"*Jah*. Rather than rent, we've had to pay for the materials for the *haus* repairs. That's come all at the same time. I know we'll save more in the long run with Levi being so generous to allow us free rent for so long."

"I didn't know things were that bad for you. I can give you some money I've saved."

Joy sniffed. *"Denke,* that's sweet of you, but we do have the money. Isaac just doesn't want to spend it. He's saving harder since he's known he's going to be a *vadder."*

"That's understandable. He wants to be a good provider."

"He's so focused on saving for a *haus* of our own. Time will run out on this place, we can't live here forever, and we'll need to be gone so Levi can find a paying tenant. Isaac said he wants the next place we live in to be our own."

"Is that what you want? Is that so important to you as well? Does it really matter?"

Joy shrugged. "I guess it is. I guess I did what I did because I just wanted something a little special. I know it was wrong. I was feeling down and I saw this in the store and wanted it so badly. I'll show you." She got up and opened a cupboard in the kitchen and came back with a finely knitted white baby dress with pink rosebuds. She handed it to Cherish. "One of the workers at the store saw me take it and called the police."

Cherish couldn't believe her ears. "The police?"

"*Jah*, I know, and then I had to call Isaac. They took me down to the police station and that's where I had to call him from."

"Oh, that's so awful, Joy." Cherish looked down at the dress and tears stung behind her eyes.

"It was the first time I ever did anything wrong and everyone found out. Other people do wrong and never get found out."

"Not everyone," Cherish said, trying to make Joy feel better.

"As well as Isaac, Christina and Mark know too."

"How? Couldn't Isaac have kept it from his *schweschder?*"

"Because I had to call Isaac while he was at work. He had to give Mark some reason that he had to leave so suddenly."

"Yeah well he could've—"

"What? Lied? I can't expect him to lie for a thief like me."

"Stop it right now! You did something bad once. You asked *Gott's* forgiveness?"

"Of course I did, Cherish."

"Did He forgive you?"

"*Jah.* He always forgives."

"There you go. Your sin is forgotten and forgiven. So, why are you so miserable? Just don't do it again and all will be fine."

Joy blew out a deep breath while Cherish took another mouthful of tea. "Isaac doesn't look at me the same. I'm just blessed that the store owner didn't want to press charges. She said I could keep the dress since I must've wanted it so bad. What a sweet woman to be kind to someone so awful." Joy picked up the dress and held it to her chest. Then she put it back down on the table.

"It is very pretty. I could've bought it for you. I have savings."

"I can never put it on my *boppli*. This dress has so many bad memories attached to it now. Isaac has lost trust in me. He probably wonders why he married me. I wonder about myself now too. What made me sin, Cherish?"

"Temptation. You wanted something pretty." Cherish grabbed it. "I'll see that you get one like this, only prettier. I'm not much good at knitting, but I'll find someone who is."

"Denke, Cherish. You've always been kind."

"I have? I mean, *jah,* I have."

Then Joy took hold of Cherish's hand and looked into her eyes. "Florence can't know, or *Mamm.* Please don't tell anyone at all. I'd never be able to look at them again."

"They won't. Don't worry, leave this to me. I'll never tell no matter what. Not even if someone tries to beat the information out of me."

That brought a smile to Joy's lips. "I don't think that will happen."

"If it does, I won't tell."

"Don't worry about finding someone to make me a dress like that. It's too pretty and it would be too prideful. *Bopplis* need to be dressed plainly just like us."

"And she could be a he and then it would be weird. So, the answer is to have the *boppli* in something pretty for home when you're not going out anywhere. That way it can't be prideful. How does that sound?"

Joy nodded. *"Denke,* Cherish. Do you think less of me now? Tell me the truth."

"Nee. I think more of you for being truthful, and showing that you're real. We all fail at things."

Joy sighed. "I think less of myself. I don't know what Isaac feels about me. He hasn't been the same to me since. He married me because he thought I was a certain way and now I've ruined everything. He can't love me now, how could he?"

339

"A wise person told me that people do disappointing things. I do them, you do them, we all do them. We can't give those things our attention."

Joy sniffed again. "I like that. Was that Aunt Dagmar who said that?"

"*Nee*. It was Levi."

"Levi?"

Cherish nodded.

"I never would've guessed."

"I was surprised too. Now, stop worrying. You did one bad thing in your life. It's not the end of your marriage. I'm sure Isaac's not perfect."

"It was something that I never would've thought of doing. I've never stolen anything in my life before now. I looked at it, I wanted it and then I knew Isaac wouldn't have been happy. That made me want it more because I couldn't have it."

"That's exactly what I've been saying to Eddie. I couldn't have said it better."

Joy tilted her head. "What does Eddie have to do with this?"

Cherish realized how unfeeling she was being to Joy. "Nothing. I'm sorry."

"Tell me."

"I'm trying to help him with Caroline. He likes her, but I said not to let her know it. She's so attractive, she's used to male attention. I told him he has to stand out by not liking her, bringing about the rule that you want what you can't have."

"It's hardly the same thing."

Cherish looked down. "I know. I wish I could take back the things that come out of my mouth sometimes. Please don't be so hard on yourself, Joy. You're so good and so perfect. You made one mistake, so what?"

Joy reached out and touched the dress once more. "It was a big mistake. I've never been so humiliated and so frightened as I was when I was waiting in the back room of the store for the police." The tears started again.

"So what?" Cherish said.

"How can Isaac love me now?"

"He does. Of course he does."

"I'm a thief."

"*Nee,* you're not. You took one thing because it was pretty."

"I wish I could go back to that time. What made me weaken?"

"The devil is always lurking, tempting us."

"Hmm. Maybe. I don't know if it's the devil or if it's me who's so awful."

"You're not. You're not. Joy, you're the best person I know. Don't let one mistake take away all the good decisions you've made, and all the sensible choices."

"I wish Isaac thought the same as you do, but how can I expect him to forgive me when I can't forgive myself? It's like someone else did it. Someone I don't even know." She stared into the distance. "What's happening to me?"

Cherish had no answers. It was awful to see Joy like this. She had to say something. "We are only human, Joy. Maybe *Gott* allowed you to make this one mistake to open your heart and so ... so you could be more compassionate to others when they succumb to temptations."

Joy turned to face Cherish. "You're right. I have been harsh in my judgements of others when I look back now."

"It's possible I'm right."

"That makes me feel better. *Gott* allowed it to happen so I can become more compassionate. I used to be judgmental of people and now I have softened. Ah, I feel better. My heart has opened to *Gott's* love."

Cherish smiled now that her sister was feeling better. "Do you think Isaac should give you a little more money?"

"*Nee*. It's not that. I don't think that's what led me to do it. It was something wrong in my head. Not so much that he keeps money from me."

"Okay. I'm glad that's sorted." Cherish nibbled on her cookie. "Now, I need your advice."

"What is it?" Joy dabbed the paper napkin under her eyes.

"Hope is upset that Fairfax has not married her right away, or set a date."

"I thought she was looking a little off lately. Not her usual happy self. So that's why?"

"That'd be it. Then, I visited him and kind of told him how she felt and he seemed to be angry, then they had a kind of a fight, or a falling out. He then told her he needed a few days to think about things. She was awfully upset thinking they might not even have a future together. He was at the house yesterday and she won't tell me what was said. I should've listened in, but *Mamm* was there so I couldn't."

"Do you think I can do something to help?"

"Maybe."

"Can you think of anything?"

"Nothing that I wouldn't get into trouble for. I was thinking if he thought she was in danger, or missing, he'd realize how much she meant to him." Cherish raised her hand when Joy looked horrified. "Don't worry, I won't do that. I already decided against it. I already watched it play out in my head and I got into terrible trouble for it."

Joy brought her fingertips to her mouth and laughed. "That's right, you would. Just pray and leave it in *Gott's* hands."

"*Jah*, but what if He wants us to do something to help them?"

"What if He doesn't? What if He wants them to find their own way around this?"

Cherish stared at Joy. She'd feel better if she did something, rather than sit around and do nothing. "Faith without works ..."

"Just don't misuse Scripture to suit yourself. We pray and then if we need to do something *Gott* will show us clearly. You don't make a plan and then think you're acting in faith when it's come from your own mind."

"Okay. I guess I see what you mean. So, you can't think of anything?"

Joy sighed. "Didn't you hear what I just said?"

"*Jah,* but ..."

"Relationships try us sometimes and that's not always a bad thing. Fairfax and Hope are going to learn a lot about each other by going through this little misunderstanding. They're going to learn how to agree and how to talk to each other when they don't agree about things."

Cherish pouted. "It all sounds a bit boring. The next thing you'll say is something about compromise."

Joy laughed.

"I don't want to compromise if I get married."

"You'll need to if you want to get married someday."

Cherish blew out a long breath. "I'll marry a man who agrees with everything I say."

"And where will you find such a man?"

"Gott will send him to me."

"He'll be a real miracle man."

Cherish put her hands over her heart. "I can't wait to meet him."

"Oh, Cherish, haven't you figured out by now such a man doesn't exist?"

"I'm believing he does."

Joy laughed. "Your visit has cheered me up. *Denke* for coming to see me. Now, have you seen the *boppli's* room lately?"

"*Nee.* I haven't been here for weeks."

"I'll show you."

Cherish followed Joy into a pale-yellow room, ready with a crib with netting over it. In the corner was a white rocking chair. "Oh, I love this chair." Cherish sat down in it.

"Isaac found it. Someone was throwing it out just because it needed painting. He brought it home, cleaned it, sanded it back and painted it, and now it's as good as new."

"I love it. He did a great job. It seems you have everything you could ever want, Joy."

Joy put her hands on her stomach. "I can't wait to meet this little one. I love him or her already."

"Me too. I'll be your *boppli's* favorite aunt. I'll make sure of it."

There was a knock on the door.

"That'll be Hope. She's early." They both walked to the front door and instead of Hope it was Bliss.

"Where's Hope?" Cherish asked.

"At home with a headache. She asked me to collect you."

"Come in, Bliss. It's so good to see you. I'll make us hot tea."

When they sat down at the table with their tea and cookies, Cherish showed Bliss the dress and told her she was going to ask Wilma if she could make one the same.

"Why not just use this dress?" Bliss asked Joy.

Joy opened her mouth and no words came out. Cherish had to jump in to save her sister. "This one is a borrowed one. It's not Joy's."

"Okay. It's very pretty."

"It's just for the *boppli* to wear at home."

"And, by the looks of this, you're hoping for a girl?" Bliss asked.

"We'll be happy with a boy or a girl. Whatever *Gott* has chosen for us. I just like the dress."

Bliss started talking to Joy and all the while, Cherish felt odd. It was as though the foundations of her world had been shaken. Joy had always been a rock—so stable, reliable, and so good. Cherish couldn't wrap her head around her sister's actions. She could only imagine Isaac would feel as though he'd had his legs kicked out from under him.

Cherish had to wonder if she could rely on anything or anyone in her life now that she knew what she did about Joy.

Wilma certainly wasn't reliable.

Favor, her closest sister had ignored her these past months, clearly preferring Caroline's company.

Florence had left them all for Carter. Now Florence only cared about Carter, her baby, apples, apple trees and the quality of soil.

Both Mercy and Honor had moved far away, and their letters were coming less and less often as time went by.

Dat had left her when he died.

Levi had nearly died, so that had left her shaken.

Bliss was nice, but she was a little bit of a traitor having unapologetically stolen Adam Wengerd from her.

Hope didn't care about anyone or anything except Fairfax, and marrying him and having dozens of *bopplis*.

The *Englisher* Cherish liked was leaving it up to her to call him, which Cherish didn't like.

She couldn't even rely on Malachi, the caretaker of her farm. He never ever followed one of her instructions.

Cherish looked up at Joy who was now talking with Bliss.

Sure, she used to roll her eyes at Joy's wholesome ways and goodness, but at the same time, Cherish had respected Joy's strength to follow *Gott's* ways.

Everything and everybody in Cherish's life was full of uncertainty.

Dat and Aunt Dagmar hadn't any choice in leaving her, but that didn't stop Cherish from feeling abandoned.

Were you officially grown up when you realized that life, and people were a disappointment?

Chapter 27

A few days passed and Hope had been worrying so much about Fairfax that she felt sick. All the stress had given her a headache, and the headache had made her nauseous. She was wandering through the apple orchard praying, holding her stomach because she was feeling poorly. When Fairfax was with her, she felt alive. When he wasn't, she felt she wasn't truly alive.

If Fairfax left her for good, she'd never love again. It would also kill her to see him with another woman. If that happened, she'd have to leave the community. It was hard to keep the fearful thoughts from her head, but the way Fairfax had acted toward her, she had little confidence things would return to normal.

"Hope."

She stopped still. It was Fairfax's voice. She turned around to see him striding toward her. Her feet started in motion, heading to him.

"What are you doing?"

She smiled. He seemed to be in a better mood. "Just walking. Why aren't you at work?"

"I've just finished the morning milking. I asked for an hour off."

"Oh."

"It's cold out here." He took his coat off and draped it around her without even asking.

That one action made her feel safe, cared for and protected. *"Denke."*

"Can we talk somewhere?" he asked, softly.

"Sure."

"Let's go back to the *haus* and sit on the porch."

She shook her head, knowing they'd be interrupted. "Shall we just walk?"

He looked up at the sky. "Sure, unless it rains."

"It won't." They started walking together and she hoped everything would be fine. He had something to say. Was he going to end things? Is that why he wanted her to go back to the house so someone would be there to comfort her when he walked away for good? "Are you cold?" she asked him.

"A little."

"Have the coat back."

"*Nee*. You keep it. I don't want you to catch a cold."

She glanced over at the trees to the left of her. When he delivered the dreaded news, she'd act like it didn't bother her. She'd wait until he drove away before she cried.

Finally, he said, "I said I wanted some days to think about things and I've taken that time. *Denke* for understanding."

She looked up at his smiling face and slowly nodded. There were no words. All she wanted was for him to say what he'd come to say. When he didn't speak, she had to. "What have you been thinking about?"

"The future."

"And?" She bit down on the inside of her mouth.

"I can see now that we are very different in our approaches to life. You thought we could just get married and then by some stroke of luck or some sprinkle of fairy dust everything would be provided for us. We have nothing, zero. I don't want to live here with your folks after we get married."

Her breath caught in her throat. He still wanted to get married if he was speaking like this. "What do you want?"

"I want to know where I'm headed. We can't marry this year because it's too soon, but Hope ..." He stopped and took hold of her hand. "Will you marry me next year?"

"Next year?"

"December 10. If that's all right with you and your folks. I've talked to the bishop about it already and he's written it down."

She stared at his smiling face and tried to hold back the tears. He'd made the effort to talk with the bishop about their marriage. If the bishop had written down the date, he must've approved the union.

He spoke again. "I know it's more than a year away, but please be patient. I do want everything to be perfect. If I've said anything other than that, I was speaking rashly and wasn't being sensible. I want to be sensible and stable for you, Hope. For you and for our *kinner.*"

Tears of joy escaped her eyes and she tried to blink them back. They weren't the sorrowful tears she had expected. "It's a perfect distance away."

He squeezed her hand. "By then we'll have a place to live and I'll have a proper job."

She couldn't help herself. She put her arms around him and hugged him. "It's perfect."

He then encircled his arms around her, holding her even closer. "You don't mind waiting? It's more than a year."

She closed her eyes as her head pressed into his shoulder. "I know. You keep saying that."

He chuckled. "I just need time to plan things. If I don't have a plan I don't feel comfortable."

Hope looked up at him. "I'm the same. I'm a planner. I thought you weren't."

His eyes opened wide as he stared into hers. "I thought *you* weren't."

"*Nee.* I am."

She could feel his body relax.

"Now that we have a date for our wedding, I need work. Proper paying work. I'm going to keep looking until I find something. Florence and Carter said they might be losing the man who works for them on my folks' old orchard. They'll find out in a couple of days if he's moving on."

"That would be perfect," she whispered, almost breathlessly.

"I know. Are you sure you don't mind waiting that long?"

"As long as we have a plan and a wedding date, then I'm happy."

"Me too."

Once again, Hope rested her head on his shoulder just as *Gott* sprinkled the first snowflakes of the season over the Baker Apple Orchard.

Thank you for reading Amish Winter of Hope.

www.SamanthaPriceAuthor.com

The next book in the series

Book 15 A Baby for Joy

The Baker Apple Orchard is finally taking shape, but not everyone is happy about it.

Cherish and the Englisher visitor are still at odds, so Cherish steps up her plan for her to fall in love with the local beekeeper. If this works, it will be one step toward getting rid of her.

Cherish is soon distracted when she decides Joy isn't as happy as she could be for a woman who's about to give birth.

Can Cherish fix Joy's problems before the baby arrives?

THE AMISH BONNET SISTERS

Book 1 Amish Mercy

Book 2 Amish Honor

Book 3 A Simple Kiss

Book 4 Amish Joy

Book 5 Amish Family Secrets

Book 6 The Englisher

THE AMISH BONNET SISTERS

Book 18 Her Amish Farm

Book 19 The Unsuitable Amish Wedding

Book 20 Her Amish Secret

Book 21 Amish Harvest Mayhem

Book 22 Amish Family Quilt

Book 23 Hope's Amish Wedding

Book 24 A Heart of Hope

Book 25 A Season for Change

Book 26 Amish Farm Mayhem

Book 27 The Stolen Amish Wedding

Book 28 A Season for Second Chances

Book 29 A Change of Heart

Book 30 The Last Wedding

Book 31 Starting Over

Book 32 Love and Cherish

Book 33 Amish Neighbors

Book 34 Her Amish Quilt

Book 35 A Home of Their Own

About Samantha Price

Samantha Price is a USA Today bestselling author of Amish romance books and cozy mysteries. She was raised Brethren and has a deep affinity for the Amish way of life, which she has explored extensively with over a decade of research.
She is mother to two pampered rescue

cats, and a very spoiled staffy with separation issues.

www.SamanthaPriceAuthor.com

Made in the USA
Monee, IL
16 May 2024

58504704R40218